HE BE DRAGONS

WAS A TRADITIONAL INDICATION BY EARLY MAP-MAKERS THAT A REGION WAS UNEXPLORED AND MIGHT HOLD TERRORS.

A TALE OF MORTALS, MYTHS AND MYSTERY

BY

ANNE WILSON

Strategic Book Publishing and Rights Co.

Book Design/Layout by Kalpart. Visit www.kalpart.com

Strategic Book Publishing and Rights Co.
12620 FM 1960, Suite A4-507
Houston TX 77065
www.sbpra.com

ISBN: 978-1-62516-172-7

For Robin who shared the adventure

To Margaret —
a good friend + neighbour
happy days!
Anne

CONTENTS

JUST BECAUSE YOU CAN'T SEE THEM

DOESN'T MEAN THEY'RE NOT THERE . . .

CHAPTER 1
ONCE UPON A TIME

The Internet Café off the Plaza Major was always busy on Saturdays. Anna could only see one vacant seat; it was opposite the man to whom something had been drawing her attention for the last few weeks. She hesitated then walked forwards.

The man was, as usual, sitting in one of the leather covered armchairs, bright slanting sunshine falling on the newspaper opened across his lap.

High overhead, old-fashioned ceiling fans re-arranged inert air and a few circling flies with a soft whirring noise. Nearby, the fronds of a large potted palm quivered slightly.

'Excuse me, is this seat taken?'

The man looked up and quickly removed a pair of reading glasses from the bridge of his nose. His eyes were a cool grey-blue, typical of northern Caucasian races.

'No, no, you must sit; please.' He sat upright, placing the hastily folded newspaper on the marble table-top and watched as Anna seated herself and leaned her shopping bags against the side of her chair.

'I have seen you working at a desk up there.' He glanced towards the café's rear, at the new mezzanine floor with de-humidified air, laminated tables and ports for lap-tops. 'You have much to do. You are a secretary or perhaps a translator?'

Anna coloured slightly at his directness, 'No, actually I'm a writer. I used to be a children's' teacher in England, now I'm a writer here in Mallorca. My apartment doesn't have air conditioning so in summer I sometimes come here to work upstairs . . . I usually shop on Saturdays.'

'So I see.' The man cast a glance across Anna's bags. 'Normally I am not to be found here on a Saturday. Today I had a purchase to make in town. My name is Nils. I am Danish. I live here in Palma. You are English, and your name is . . . ?'

Café life revolved around them; people chattered, plates clattered, bistro chair-feet scraped scuffed marble tiles and waiters wove in and out with practised verve. In the streets outside, pavements and motionless date palms baked in the dazzling glare as the midday sun blazed over everything, slowing time and motion.

Anna too experienced a strange slewing sensation of sound and colour, as if something else had slowed, held its breath and paused to listen as she answered the stranger's questions.

***

The Dragon sitting beside the potted palm moved closer. He took an interest in the lives of a great many humans, with their brief life spans, their circadian rhythms. Their auras fascinated him, but there were always those who interested him more than others.

He had tracked Nils' aura from Denmark's northern waters to the Balearics along Hitler's

Atlantic Wall, an ancient Viking route, which ended at Es Trenc on the north-facing side of Mallorca. However, he knew too long spent in temperate zones intensified the mouldering algal smell that emanated from his grey scaly skin, risked it permeating the shimmering layers that separated him from human vision. No one had ever seen him except in dreams, but some warm blooded creatures had come close.

***

Anna glanced around the café and lifted tendrils of damp hair away from her cheeks and forehead to allow cooling perspiration to chill the surface of her skin. She saw that quite a few seats were actually available, the nearest being just two tables away. She frowned slightly, wondering what had made her think she'd claimed the only one.

'This cafeteria is very popular.' The stranger leaned forward, giving away no awareness of her momentary confusion. 'And your writing; it is academic?' He smiled encouragingly.

'No, I'm writing my third children's story.' Anna relaxed back into her chair and sipped her coffee.

'Ah, then you are a lady Roald Dahl?'

'Not exactly, I'm probably more of a lady Hans Christian Andersen. You know, Once upon a time, that sort of thing.' Anna congratulated herself silently on having come up with the name of the Danish storyteller, a countryman of this new acquaintance.

'Oh surely not . . . a most unfortunate man, a tormented soul who died a virgin. We will hope the Fates are kinder to you. But what is your story?'

Making a mental note to research Hans Christian Andersen, Anna replied; 'Well, it's a sort of fairy tale with a dragon in it. I'm basing my characters on some larger-than-life characters here on the island. I'm attempting some illustrations too, but I'm having difficulty developing the right sort of dragon. At the moment, my biggest problem's his home. I can't visualise him inside his cave.'

Her new companion paid careful attention, nodding slightly. 'But the Caves of the Dragon are here on this island.'

'The famous Cuvas Del Drac, I know. I thought they'd inspire me but they're too cavernous, too brightly lit and too full of tourists. I think my dragon needs his space to be smaller, more personal.'

Nils' focus slipped away into the middle distance; Anna sipped her coffee and brushed imaginary crumbs off her lap, offering a vague smile to no one in particular.

***

The Dragon waited. Human life was like a story in a book; he could put it down then return and pick up the thread. He could manipulate the characters, finding his way into their psyche through the vulnerability of an emotional crisis or a chink in their armour, a fault-line in their veneer of civilisation.

A servant of fate, he nudged the moving finger, that which writes and having writ moves on.

***

Nils' focus swung back. 'Some of my favourite ancestors, the Vikings, knew of dragons. They journeyed where the faint-hearted dared not go; into unmapped regions of land and water. And my home is a Spanish cave-house.'

'I've heard of those . . . but you said you lived here in Palma.'

'The backdrop to the harbour front here is a high rock face, obscured by fanciful, over-priced commercial properties; a monument to the greed of property developers.'

'Yes . . . ?'

'A sliver of it is owned by me, a terraced frontage built high up onto a cave entrance. I bought it some years ago, before much of the recent development. My brother Erik assisted me in making improvements and excavating further back. It is sandwiched now between a large hotel and a nightclub.'

'It sounds fascinating; I can't imagine it.' Anna tried and failed to conjure up a mental picture of the dwelling Nils was describing.

She had been distracted by his presence in the café for a while now but had never expected to meet or speak to him. She judged him to be at least ten years older than herself, but in a way she found quite attractive.

He always sat alone, always claimed one of the large leather sofas, although she couldn't recall ever seeing him walking either in or out through the door. He studied the daily broadsheets, only occasionally looking up to glance around. His thick white hair, neat spade-shaped goatee and strong square features certainly did look Scandinavian, or at least the way Anna imagined a Scandinavian might look; healthy, vital, fair-skinned and tanned. She couldn't actually recall having met one before.

Nils was speaking again. ‘So, our meeting is surely fate. You must visit my home and see for yourself. It is not much but we will have lunch on the terrace. You must see I have the best view in the whole of Palma. Tomorrow is Sunday, you will come . . . for your dragon? Have you a car?’

‘No. I’m sorry, I don’t drive.’ Anna always cringed slightly at this admission; too lazy to learn, too hard-up to afford the finance, too comfortable relying on others? How did people interpret it and why was she apologising? Maybe she was just doing her bit to save the planet.

Nils raised his eyebrows. ‘So, no matter. You have paper to write the bus numbers which stop nearby, together with directions for finding me? I must leave you as I have an errand here in town, but tomorrow I will make preparations. I will be waiting. We will discuss your fantasy.’

‘Please don’t go to any trouble.’ Anna burrowed in her bag for her notebook and pen. Her hands were clammy. Why on earth did she keep so much rubbish in every bag she owned?

‘On ordinary days I do not encourage visitors, but I am, as I believe you say, too much set in my ways. Your company will be good for me.’

Nils leaned across and politely took Anna’s notebook and pen, wrote down some directions and sketched a rudimentary map. He added a phone number. ‘You must meet Tosca and Puccini.’

Before Anna could reply, he stood, almost to attention, leant towards her and extended his hand in a brief handshake. His palm was dry and cool.

'Just so, we are friends who will meet tomorrow.'

Then, with a courteous bow of his head her new acquaintance turned and left through the open café doors.

Anna watched until the blue and white of his checked shirt was lost amongst the weft and warp of city life as it threaded its way in and out along hot streets. Palm fronds wafted imperceptibly in the huge planter behind her seat; time's equilibrium was restored.

She sank back into her chair. The timbre of Nils' voice had a hypnotic quality. His slightly accented words repeated themselves in her head like an incantation; *Tosca and Puccini?*

***

By the time Nils reached the Ramblas, the Dragon had already returned to his natural habitat, to the chilling brilliance of the northern waters, his recent journey a success. Now he skimmed up the straits of the Skagerrak and beyond to set the seal of fate on a group of illegal and brutal fur trappers operating out near Svalbard.

Soon, due to their unfortunate accident and with their pitiless disregard for the suffering of other species ended, their bodies would be stacked up neatly, awaiting burial. They would remain there until spring when the ground thawed sufficiently to allow the town's inhabitants to inter their dead.

***

Anna studied Nils' handwriting. It was unembellished, bold and confident. She remembered the design on a beautiful Icelandic sweater he had worn sometime during the winter months.

What was it his cologne made her think of? Ozone from the sea, surf foaming on a beach, wind chimes tinkling somewhere; or was that ice in a glass? Duck-egg coloured sky, in England, no, not in England... Anna closed her eyes; the coffee machine hissed out a burst of steam, long grasses swished softly in a light breeze; tall flower stems bent their heads towards her; she heard whispering...

A heavily laden housewife dropped into the seat Nils had just vacated. Anna opened her eyes, detected the pungent smell of fish from the woman's carelessly wrapped parcels and saw a plastic carrier containing leaking newsprint. With a quick smile she gathered up her shopping and followed Nils out onto the street.

The day had acquired a different vitality. Nils had mentioned no wife or partner. He reminded her a little of the headmaster of a school she had taught in once, Broadway Comprehensive, Mr Lovatt, someone with whom she had misguidedly had a brief affair. She recalled how aroused she had been after sitting beside him through an entire school production of A Mid-summer Night's Dream; their thighs pressed together in the semi-darkness, blood pumping, adrenalin flowing. The memory came now from somewhere long ago. She pushed it away.

Nils hadn't exactly invited her on a date, had he? But she did find him attractive and intriguing. Could he really be living alone in a home which might be inspirational for her dragon's cave?

To capture the imagination of younger readers she had endowed her dragon with a shy disposition, an unmade bed and a large cupboard filled with interesting treasures beginning with the letter 'B'. She had named him Trog. Trog grew up during the story but still inhabited the same cave. Perhaps at last she would be better able to describe and draw his home. Filled with anticipation, she pondered what a strange thing fate was.

It was siesta time as Anna boarded the bus to return to her apartment. City streets were sapped of life. The last remaining metal shutters rattled down over shop fronts and all activity ceased as buildings fell into a communal slumber. Traffic intermittently roared away from crossings on orange lights, and the bus followed in its wake, laboriously grinding its gears. Trails of exhaust fumes hung suspended, fouling the humid air and eddying round the broad leaves of rubber trees lining the dusty carriageway. A few beady-eyed pigeons patrolled the empty pavements, their progress watched by scrawny feral cats stalking the back streets.

***

Now, less than twenty-four hours later, feeling on the edge of an adventure, Anna waited at the bus stop for the number three Palma bus which would take her through the labyrinthine area of Terreno to find a cave-house and a stranger named Nils. Her imagination rambled; he wouldn't have forgotten, would he? What if she couldn't find the address? What if she found it and he wasn't there? Why did she feel so nervous and why had she still not found an effective anti-perspirant in all this heat?

An opaque doppelganger returned her gaze from a nearby shop window; a reflected image which never quite matched the one in her imagination, was somehow never quite what she expected to see. A person of average height and average build with shortish, light brown, lightly permed hair. A woman of almost forty who could still pass for early thirties; could in fact pass as anyone, couldn't she? She had a figure; possibly a little thicker than it had been a few years ago, but who would know? She had no history on this island, only, she hoped, a future waiting to be written.

She used to wonder who she could have been but accepted herself now. But how, in this cosmopolitan city, did she manage to look so English? Clothes here were a confused mix of fabulous, fashionable, fake and retro, especially among ex-pats. The Spanish always looked annoyingly stylish and . . . very Spanish, whereas most of the Brits seemed to be having an identity crisis; something to do with the climate, obviously.

Her feet made unattractive sticky noises inside her new leather sandals as she tried to stand in the shade, hoping her bag held everything she might need, except that she had no idea what today would bring. She had decided her lap-top would look too business-like and less friendly so had brought instead a notebook and pen, sketchbook and pencil, and had liberally applied her favourite scent by Jo Malone. She reminded herself her interest was supposed to lie more in the cave-house than in its occupant, but scent evaporated more quickly in the heat.

The bus, nearly empty at this time of day, arrived fifteen minutes late. It had a surly driver and unforgiving wooden seats, almost as if it would have preferred one not to travel at all and perhaps be contented with one's existing surroundings. On arrival at the city outskirts it grudgingly hauled its few passengers away from deserted tree-lined streets and upward into Terreno, the district overlooking the Bay of Palma, from where the winding road began its descent into the heart of the city. Up here, small local businesses thrived in a maze of alleyways, oblivious to showy markers of wealth below, where, beyond gently bobbing masts and rigging, the sea glittered all the way to the horizon.

As Anna stepped from the bus in an area unused to unescorted, fair-skinned women, sly eyes of Hispanic residents shifted sideways registering their disapproval. Ignoring them and trying to look as if she knew where she was going, she concentrated on following Nils' directions.

To the left, dark-eyed youths loitered in deep shade beneath corridors of sheets, tablecloths, trousers and t-shirts which hung flat and lifeless above their heads. From the right, musky, spicy smells drifted from the Chinese quarter where, sitting on the pavement, two monstrous red and gold dragons guarded a gaudy-looking entrance fringed with lanterns.

Anna glanced again at the map Nils had drawn. Where was the unmarked alleyway; an opening between the barred doors of a night-club and a closed tapas bar? It must be the one in front of her. She stepped towards it. High walls on either side were tagged with snatches of graffiti; to the uninitiated, loud-looking, angry and aggressive.

The passageway narrowed gradually, sloping sharply down in the direction of the sea-front. Pink and apricot bracts of bougainvillea snaked and tumbled down from above, hindering progress, catching at hair and pricking bare shoulders with hidden thorns. Oblique shafts of sunlight cut a sharp geometric pattern of light and shade across the walls and highlighted dust motes suspended in the air.

As the passage veered sideways and the gradient steepened, two people could not have passed without touching, and this thought quickened Anna's pace until she could hear her heartbeat as she listened for the scuffling of litter being disturbed either from behind or coming towards her. As dry dusty rubbish multiplied underfoot, Anna recognised the arching yellow 'M' of meals eaten and forgotten, reassuringly familiar in this unfamiliar place.

The route snaked ahead until, to her relief, Anna identified the sturdy forged gate which blocked a narrow entrance. Just as Nils had described it, it was set into lofty plastered walls of dirty white and grey stone. Beneath a rusted letter-box, an equally rusted padlock hung loose. Had he recently unlocked it to admit a special guest?

In response to a firm push, the gate ground open, woken from its hot dry slumber. Anna winced as the noise broke the silence of the siesta, announcing her arrival. She stepped gingerly across the threshold, half turning to close the gate behind her.

Was she trespassing? Had she entered the right property? Where was her enigmatic host? Was she wearing too much perfume? Her bare skin tingled with fresh perspiration. Why did this visit feel like something illicit and dangerous?

CHAPTER 2
THE CAVE-HOUSE

Three stone steps took Anna up onto a broad terrace paved with cracked grey flagstones. She saw she was high above the Paseo Maritimo, looking out over much of the city of Palma and its bay beyond. A dazzling vista of crowded sun-bleached and white-walled blocks, pantiled, domed and flat rooftops. And a million balconies, with here and there tiny parasols of palm and ficus. The bay blended aquamarine hues into the cobalt distance where ferries and tankers in faraway shipping lanes shimmered like a mirage anchored in hot blue space. Only when she finally exhaled did Anna realise she had found the view to be truly breathtaking.

A sudden movement at the terrace's far end broke the spell. Nils appeared through open French doors which were set in the back wall beyond two shuttered windows which looked like closed eyes cut into the cliff.

'Well done! You have found me. I have been most impatient.'

He beckoned his guest towards him and greeted her with a kiss on each cheek. Was this, Anna wondered, Danish tradition or a personal touch conveniently borrowed from the emotionally demonstrative Spanish?

'Please, you must make yourself at home.'

'Thank you, this is . . . amazing.'

Nils invited her to select a comfortable seat, then turned back towards the shaded interior, where he could be glimpsed pouring Spanish Cava into glasses placed on a low table.

A set of moulded and weathered plastic chairs sat unevenly on the terrace's old tiles. A worn moquette settee was placed under a faded sunshade, and a low stone bench, built into an arbour on the end wall near the French doors, was overhung with a delicate water-fall of liana vines which curled and trailed their pink fluted flowers down from obscured heights above.

On seeing Nils was advancing with a tray, Anna settled herself on a cushioned seat in front of an old wooden table, the surface of which was scrubbed and smooth, its colour leached by the elements to a silvery ash.

Over the terrace's crumbling parapet, far down below, the route of the promenade, the grand Paseo Maritimo, traced the harbour wall. It was marked from above by glossy dark green rubber trees, between which passing traffic glinted sporadically. Muted sound drifted upwards. It was as if the city was humming a secret rhythm, thought Anna; the rhythm of life. It sounded different to how she remembered the rhythm of English cities, significantly without the slushing sound of tyres travelling over wet tarmac.

Scattered around the terrace, cracked terracotta pots stood in plots of baked red earth. Their over-grown foliage burgeoned haphazardly towards the sky, stray roots escaping to straggle downwards in search of water. Beside limestone walls, small geckos darted on clumsy-looking toes and scarlet hibiscus flowers unfurled tissue-like petals, reaching out with long, slim, pollen-tipped stamens. From beneath the moquette settee, a black cat watched the newcomer through half-closed eyes, whiskers twitching as she savoured a new scent in the air.

'Ah, there is Tosca.' Nils set down the tray of drinks and a simple lunch. Danish Havarti cheese, thin slices of cured ham, pickled herrings, sharp green olives, locally baked bread and a pot of aioli, the delicious garlic flavoured mayonnaise. There was also an imported butter pat wrapped in familiar silver foil.

'I have also a little black dog, Puccini; he lives on the rooftops. He sleeps during the siesta.'

Sitting down, Nils gestured vaguely above himself, where ramshackle and apparently deserted constructions balanced on ledges against the sloping cliff, clinging below the distant backs of the alleyways high up above.

'It's very interesting here.' Anna glanced briefly upwards and quickly dismissed thoughts of the implications of a landslide.

Nils passed her a plate. 'But I hope you are hungry at this time of day. Please help yourself, there is Danish butter. I have plenty, although not usually such a beautiful visitor to share it with. Skål!'

'Thank you for lunch, and the compliment. Skål!'

Anna raised her glass and sneaked a look at her new companion, wondering who he was and how he came to be here. In his unbuttoned raw linen shirt, sleeves neatly rolled to reveal muscled forearms and a virile spring to his thick white hair, he definitely struck her as an attractive man. She glimpsed a tanned body with just a little greying chest hair. Practical Khaki shorts, belted with a worn leather belt with a silver buckle, and a worn pair of Birkenstocks, which Anna had always called Jesus sandals, completed the picture.

'You have family here?' His tone was casual, his body language relaxed. He selected a pickled herring and broke off a chunk of bread.

'No, I'm alone. After both my parents died I inherited their holiday apartment here. I came to sort it out and had an epiphany; a "now or never" sort of thing. I gave up my teaching job in England; everyone was worrying about cut-backs and redundancies. I sold my flat there and planned to live on the proceeds in the apartment here, buying time to write. Thank goodness my first two stories are proving popular, so I'm able to stay here, and now I'm working on a third one. If that does well I'll move to a better apartment and carry on writing. I'd love to live here in Palma. There's so much life and colour everywhere.'

Nils listened carefully. 'Continue, please.'

Anna self-consciously sipped her wine. 'I've made some good friends, ex-pats mainly. We meet up in a restaurant every two or three weeks and swap news and gossip. I'd miss them a lot if I went back to England.'

'I too have many acquaintances here. My family is now only my brother in Denmark, Erik. He is a veterinarian in Copenhagen. He used to come here every year to cycle around the island before . . . but not so now. You have no children?'

'No.' Anna was used to a silence following this reply to this question, as if there was nowhere to go from there. With no pets either, she sometimes felt somehow lacking, apologetic even. She did like children, didn't she? Did that count? Nils however appeared perfectly satisfied with the situation, regarding her steadily with an undecipherable expression in his eyes.

Their meal was enjoyed slowly as they watched the sun slide sideways across the bay. As the heat softened and the first edges of shadows began to appear, Anna's curiosity about the interior of the cave-house re-awakened. After all, she told herself, this was her mission as a writer and she wanted to remember and to note and sketch as much as possible. She suggested it might be comfortable to sit inside in the shade.

'But of course. Mi cueva es tu cueva, my cave is your cave. Please . . . '

Nils smiled, extending an arm towards the tall glazed doors which seemed the only access to the dwelling hewn from the rock-face rising behind them. So between the parched streets of Terreno above and the turquoise pool of a front-line hotel far down below, Anna entered Nils' private kingdom.

The inner space was furnished with two beige-coloured settees, each draped with cream coloured cotton throws. A small television and an old fashioned Bakelite telephone sat on a low table. Behind this arrangement a kitchen area was laid out to the left and, further back, to the right was a dining area. The dining table had a typewriter on the nearside, and behind the table, the distinctively lacquered black and scrolled gold of an old treadle sewing machine shone dimly. This had a work in progress, what looked like a large white sheet, which lay partly across the table. A headless tailor's dummy stood in a dark recess. Still further back was a door-sized aperture, partly obscured by a draped curtain, around which the edge of a bed was visible.

Books, journals and magazines competed for space on most of the available surfaces. As Anna's eyes adjusted, she could see the kitchen looked clean and functional, worktops and hanging utensils shining in the half-light. There was some sort of coffee machine and a few modern looking bowls and gadgets. On the nearest work bench sat an olive wood bowl heaped with bright citrus fruits.

Nils advanced to the dining table and whipped away the sheet with a flourish, allowing it to settle over the dummy, whose mute presence Anna found a little unnerving. Her host indicated a chair and she sat obediently, looking around herself. There were no pictures on the walls but perhaps they wouldn't hang well on plastered rock.

Soon an aroma of freshly brewing coffee quickened her senses. 'I'm sorry, but I need the bathroom. Where is it?' She looked apprehensively towards shadowy corners and the draped curtain.

'Of course, of course, you must make yourself at home. I am an old goat, unused to guests. Please forgive me.'

Nils directed her around the curtain and, stalked by the black cat Tosca, Anna crossed what did turn out to be the bedroom. She guessed this space had been hastily tidied of its owner's more personal belongings, making her think of an empty stage waiting for the play to begin. The centrepiece was a high king-sized bed. She stared at it for a moment.

An old Florentine mirror the size of a door was propped against one wall. It reflected the room's uneven dimensions and textured surfaces, lending them a curious lustre. Light from a church candle flickering in a wall sconce scattered constellations around the chamber from the mirror's pitted silvering.

Carefully sidestepping boxes piled before curtained alcoves, Anna reached a further curtain concealing the entrance to the bathroom. Here, as in the kitchen area, the rock walls were smoothly plastered. They had been glossed a mint green colour. Overhead strip-lighting glanced off white enamel facilities: washbasin, bidet and lavatory. A shower cubicle was curtained in a design Anna recognised as one of IKEA's. Towels hung folded, pristine white. The effect was functional, a little austere and essentially masculine.

The existence of further space beyond the bathroom was suggested by a custom-built, low wooden door set into the uneven wall. Fuelled by curiosity, Anna gripped the tarnished door-knob and twisted it. Stiffly resistant at first, it released suddenly. The widening aperture allowed trapped humid air to escape through the room, dragging impenetrable darkness forwards with it.

Anna drew back, closing the door as soundlessly as possible, the door-knob strange in her hand. Aware of a change to the sanitised bathroom smell as it mingled with something unidentifiable, she decided some kind of store-room would not be very interesting anyway.

When she re-joined Nils, coffee waited in a white china cup, together with scented golden slices of Spanish membrillo.

'I've always meant to try that. I know it's made from fruit; is it quince?'

'Ah yes. The golden apple, given by Paris to Aphrodite.'

‘Do you like the Greek myths?’

‘I am more familiar with Norse legend and culture, of course. Together with a business partner, I have a Danish restaurant which also caters for local Spanish tastes. Membrillo is very popular.’

‘Oh, you didn’t say you had a restaurant. Is that a wine cellar at the back of the bathroom?’

‘Yes,’ Nils answered with a slight frown. ‘There is wine in there, yes.’ He paused as if thinking. ‘Do you perhaps like Danish food? It is very healthy.’

Anna hastily dismissed a vision of Danish pastries and admitted she didn’t know.

Nils described the restaurant of which he was part owner. His partner and restaurant manager was a man called Holger Trautmann who Anna would meet if she agreed to an invitation there for dinner the following Friday. Anna readily agreed and her mind wandered as she wondered what she would wear.

Meanwhile, wine glasses were replenished and Nils laced their coffee with Spanish brandy as they settled and re-settled closer and closer on one of the couches. Shadows merged silently on the terrace outside.

Lapses in conversation were comfortable as Nils’ choice of operatic arias rose around the chamber, swelling then falling away into hidden corners. Fingers of soft Mediterranean night gradually slipped from the terrace into the room, and far below, Palma slowly turned into a richly jewelled cape thrown around the bay beneath a dark velvet sky.

The dreamy atmosphere was disturbed by a phone call to tell them Anna’s taxi was waiting by the entrance to the alleyway. Nils rose, took her hand and walking slightly in front with a powerful torch, he lead their way back up to the street above.

His brief kiss goodnight sought her lips in a measured yet powerful advance. It ignited something dormant, betrayed by her response, and Anna knew the sensation would keep her awake then disturb her dreams. He opened the car door, ushered her in, handed money to the driver and melted back into shadow so swiftly that there was no one there to wave at as the taxi pulled away.

Anna stared through her own reflection into the darkened recesses of shop doorways and deserted streets. Unlike in the city, no one here had business at this hour.

***

Back home, unable to sleep, Anna sat in bed sketching a cave and making notes.

Her small apartment block was in the increasingly unfashionable area at the back of Palma Nova. It hid its shabby facade behind a fuchsia coloured cladding of bougainvillea, threaded through with thick black loops of electric cable.

Anna liked the fact that hers was the fourth floor, which was the top, even though the old block was lacking a lift.

During the day the shrill chirr of cicadas in the surrounding shrubbery reached fever pitch. At night, nameless things scurried across the flat roof and night-things screeched. Feral cats hunted who-knew-what in the darkness below. Pine cones dropped onto the balcony and the bougainvillea rustled like pages turned by an invisible hand.

Short winters were cold; the peak of summers too hot. Sometimes the water supply faltered and occasionally the electricity mysteriously cut itself off, but life continued unfazed. Outside by day, neighbours chattered to each other in patois Spanish, their faces and those of their children always friendly. The corner *Supermercado* stocked local produce and from Anna's balcony a sea view was just visible, sparkling between overhanging pine branches and intervening rooftops.

She often reflected that one day, when she could afford to move a little up-market, she would remember this writer's den under the overhanging old pine branches with affection.

For now, following today's adventure, her mind was divided between wanting to drift and savour the warm excitement of her new friendship and a desire to celebrate the apparent lifting of her writer's block with an inspired bout of writing and sketching. Her idea seemed to have worked. At last she could see her dragon.

Rather larger and not quite as she had imagined, he seemed to be travelling towards her from a frozen north.

***

His domain stretched behind him where giant ice flows creaked and cracked constantly in a vast white silence. He had followed strong currents flowing fast and deep beneath ice fields where the snow-crust glittered like lakes of diamonds and great glaciers loomed blue and black under an unearthly arctic moon. He rode the turbulence of the mighty West winds, journeying alone, sweeping down through the northern hemisphere, down across the continent of Europe until the Earth grew too warm.

Under cover of darkness, his contours shape-shifted; his skin the colour of dull cold steel, its surface glimmering; his eyes a pale stormy flicker.

As Anna slipped deeper into sleep she found herself taken with him to the back of his cave. Gnarled, scaled fingers carefully opened the door of his large cupboard of interesting treasures beginning with 'B'.

Slowly, framed in branches and briar roses, a landscape was revealed. Black birds flew upwards; ravens, and with them, white seagulls. Butterflies hovered over banks of deep blue flowers, amongst which bees hummed, one flying outwards and into the cave. In the foreground, beetles crawled across a Bible and a bulging brown bag. In the picture plane bats began to gather, jostling and rustling.

***

Immobilised in that surreal state somewhere between sleep and wakefulness, Anna's eyes tried to focus on something nearby resembling a tall shrouded figure. Then fully awake, she recognised familiar shadows in her room. Pressing her eyes shut again, she drew up the bedcover, holding it tightly until morning slid between the slats of the shutters.

CHAPTER 3
THE WICKED QUEEN

Max and Sylvia Gold had, unbeknown to them, been immortalised as the first of the characters in Anna's book; the Wicked Queen and her husband, The King. They lived in a penthouse which topped the most exclusive block in the port, boasting unrivalled views over a picturesque marina in front and, at the rear, a backdrop of private villas on the pebbled, scrubby hillside.

Anna came each Monday to clean and tidy their apartment before the midday sun turned this activity into much harder work. She had taken two weekly domestic jobs to supplement her limited resources, which included a small advance on her book and which still earned her the smile of her bank manager, but only just.

The Wicked Queen was, as usual, imperious and unwelcoming as she admitted Anna through the wrought-iron security gate opposite the lift cage. Inside the apartment, a green fitted carpet led along the hallway into a main living area where, at the first whiff of intruders, Bijoux, the Gold's bad tempered French poodle retreated behind her mistress, yapping hysterically.

'Begin in here please. I have to go out.' Sylvia swept Bijoux into her arms and headed for the bedroom.

Anna collected her housekeeper's box of dusters and polishes and dusted and polished while Her Majesty was getting ready.

Fine gold embellishment on a magnificent collection of porcelain gleamed behind the locked glass doors of a display cabinet. The reflective surface of the imposing mahogany table, no longer used for dining in style, was a careless repository for medicinal supplements, toiletries, trivia and any recent purchases. A portrait in oils of the Gold's only son dominated the room from above an ornate mahogany sideboard which was home to bottles, decanters and trays of glasses. His arrested gaze still appeared to follow her movements, in spite of a fatal overdose having resulted in his body being recovered from a drainage dyke near Amsterdam five years earlier. Local papers had reported the tragedy with relish in both English and Spanish.

Four heavy carved turtles rested on Wilton green carpet. They supported a glass coffee table-top where overflowing ashtrays contributed to the stale air, which remained stagnant even with the French windows thrown open to a gentle Mediterranean breeze from the rooftop. An eerie feeling pervaded the room, a time warp in which ashtrays replenished themselves as soon as the watcher's back was turned and pot plants wilted in depression. Trailing gauze curtains stirred restlessly, causing pale shadows to wax and wane.

'Anna, can you come here for a minute?!' Sylvia called from the bedroom to give instructions on her choice of fresh bed linen. She was leaving to go shopping.

How could anyone sleep in here? Layers of fussily frilled, floral nylon curtains obscured the windows, but this was the penthouse; no one could see in. Body odour hung thickly in the air, mingled with Sylvia's cloying perfume; there was always an elegantly shaped bottle of it on the dressing table, Shalimar by Guerlain. It permeated the floral sheets and pillowcases, marked 'Harrods' next to their washing instructions. Lots of things, including carpet slippers and the bedside rugs on which they sat, boasted the distinctive green logo. Fitted carpets, incongruous in Spain, echoed the colour.

'These sheets are for the bed; that pile is for the wash. Please disturb my husband as little as possible, he's in the study, he's feeling rather unwell. I may not be back before you leave, so take your money; you'll find an envelope with your name on it on the dining table. It brings you up to date. Make yourself a sandwich if you wish. I'm taking Bijoux with me.' Bijoux regarded Anna with pink watery eyes, and gave a small warning 'Yip'. Even the dog's curly, truffle-coloured fur gave off a hint of Shalimar as his mistress whisked him past.

'Yes Mrs Gold.'

Five minutes later, the hollow clang of the lift's doors and the whirring reverberations of its descent could be heard in the apartment as the Wicked Queen left to pursue her unknown private life. Anna could hear she was, once again, accompanied by a disembodied male voice whose owner she must have encountered on the landing, but at whom Bijoux did not bark.

Below in the port, exclusive boutiques, expensive restaurants, up-market estate agents and agencies selling yachts and speedboats competed for business. On approaching and leaving the Gold's apartment block, Anna always imagined she was crossing a glamorous film set where shop fronts were mere facades behind which cunningly hidden sound and lighting crews, cameramen and whole wardrobe departments functioned from within giant Winnebagos.

In harsh contrast to the stylish surroundings, the Gold's rooftop terrace was carpeted in livid green Astroturf, its spikey synthetic texture coarse and unnatural. It did however appear to fool Bijoux, who left sticky brown patches which had to be rinsed away with disinfectant.

'Can you come and help me with this?' Max Gold's voice was plaintive.

Anna followed him into the cluttered kitchen. It was vented but windowless and oppressive. Anna had originally wondered why such an expensively appointed apartment had such a claustrophobic kitchen. It had taken her weeks before the penny had dropped; people like the Golds were expected to dine out all the time.

This morning the Wicked Queen had left her husband to prepare his own breakfast and the microwave had burnt the currants in his teacake. Anna directed him to the toaster. He stood watching her wash up while he waited. The silence between them was always amicable, probably due to a shared relief that his wife had left the building.

Unlike his wife, who was short and well padded, Max Gold was a tall gaunt man. Heavy investment in property development during the eighties package holiday boom had made the couple celebrities on the island. They were involved in the design and rise of some of the biggest hotels along its Southern coastline, facilitating tourism and generating employment. Now with their heyday over, their celebrity was forgotten and their friends were few, fading away as fast as his hair and her figure.

'Do you drink whisky? When you've finished today, will you stay and have a glass with me?'

Anna was aware Max drank in the daytime but he had never requested she join him before. Whisky at lunchtime, in this heat! She looked up uncertainly, feeling some sympathy for this ageing, evidently depressed and lonely man.

'Oh . . . yes, thank you.' She attempted to inject some polite enthusiasm into her voice. What on earth would they talk about? What could they possibly have in common? How quickly could one decently drink a glass of whisky? At what time might the Wicked Queen return?

'Just come into the snug when you've finished . . . er . . . that.' Max's voice tailed away down the hallway as he disappeared with his teacake, ice-cubes clinking in his tumbler.

An hour later, Anna approached the study armed with a duster. All morning her thoughts had been drifting around her previous day's visit to Nils. Now she marshalled them back into her present environment, clearing her throat as she tapped lightly on the half-closed study door.

Max was seated in the green leather wing chair which bore a permanent imprint of his slumped figure. He sat gazing out across the Mediterranean, his drink perched amongst a clutter of ornaments on the window ledge.

'Sit there.' He nodded at the seat opposite, waving the duster away with one hand and proffering a glass into which he had poured a generous measure of whisky with the other. Anna took the glass from him and he gestured vaguely to a decanter of water on a side table, then leant back in his chair with a defeated air.

Anna sat, trying to imagine him and Sylvia in the evenings, seated in chairs separated by Bijoux's basket, indifference, or perhaps hostility, charging the air around them.

Much of the wall space in here was lined with books; the diversity of the randomly placed subject matter made Anna think of unsolicited 'Readers Digest' selections, something with which she had been targeted in the past, back home in England. Framed posters advertising West End theatre productions adorned walls discoloured by years of cigarette smoke. Small photographs, many black and white, jostled for space. Some bore vaguely familiar famous faces. The face that appeared in the oil painting above the mahogany sideboard was featured; here a child, building sandcastles, there a young man posing in a black gown and mortarboard. A coloured photograph in the forefront was of Bijoux playing with a ball. Everything, including Max, looked tired and dated to Anna.

'Tell me something about yourself,' Max invited.

Bit late for an interview, thought Anna taking a sip from her glass. You employ me because I'm English, I was recommended by a mutual acquaintance, and I charge cheap rates.

'I think I've already told you; I was a children's teacher in England but I dreamed of a writing career. Inheriting my parent's apartment brought me over here and it felt like an opportunity.'

It sounded so simple, summed up like that. Max couldn't know how adrift she'd felt. The boundaries in her life had gradually disintegrated as her parents had both died within the space of a year; her father following a series of strokes and her mother of a sudden fatal heart attack. She'd had to deal, alone, with all their affairs. Life's goalposts had shifted, her ambitions seemed hollow and all of a sudden she felt she had nothing in common with her colleagues at work. Socialising had become meaningless and awkward. Distant relatives were too distant and a recent rocky relationship . . . not distant enough.

She remembered her flight to Mallorca, strapped in her seat, numbed and miserable. But the minute she stepped outside the plane in Palma airport, the warm scented air whispered enticingly. It spoke of tomorrows as yet unimagined, a blank page waiting to be written. The ratchets of the wheel of fate cranked soundlessly as she stepped down onto the tarmac.

Her employer was watching her.

'A teacher . . . no husband?' Max made his own assumptions. 'Why do you clean, you don't seem to enjoy it? What else do you do?'

Anna tried to appear a little more interesting. 'I've had two children's books published. Now I'm writing a third one with a dragon in it and I need a few extra funds to live on in the meantime.'

'It's been done already . . . the dragon thing.' Max gazed at the ceiling. 'What do you think I should do?'

'What do you mean, exactly?' Anna took another sip from her glass.

'There seems nothing left for me to do. I'm old and quite unwell . . . or so they tell me. I've decided . . . perhaps . . . I might be ready to die.' His voice was a monotone, his tanned and livered hands steady in spite of the whisky. His words hung in the air. 'I wanted to know if someone young like you could think of any reasons for me still to want to embrace life.'

'Have you talked to Mrs Gold?'

'She doesn't care. Actually, my demise would suit her very well. I think I stand in the way of certain plans of hers.'

'What about your friends?' Anna wondered what she was supposed to say. He must have drunk more than she thought. She attempted to lighten the atmosphere which was constricting her throat, making the raw spirit burn on its way down. 'Perhaps you should get a girlfriend.'

Max simply smiled a tired smile, his eyes unfocused through smudged glasses. 'I've tried that a number of times . . . and I too have written a book.'

'Was it an autobiography? How fascinating, you must have so much to tell.' Was she babbling?

'No one's interested anymore.' Max's voice remained unemotional. 'I just wondered if someone like you had any different ideas.'

Evidently, she hadn't. The question was, was he serious? Surely not. Anna left the building a little while later, her thoughts racing. Oblivious to the smell of stale perfume in the lift, the ground beneath her feet, the sun's glare on unprotected skin and eyes, she headed for the bus stop.

Who to alert to Max's state of mind, if not his wife? Also, what if she repeated their conversation and he denied everything, making her look hysterical and foolish? How was it her business, anyway?

Her route to the bus stop circled the towering apartment block where the back wall of shuttered service windows cast stretching shadows; black laser-sharp shapes dividing the baking pavement with a sudden chill. Today the sudden plunge in temperature seemed doom-laden. Anna walked faster and was relieved by the sight of a bus approaching through the dusty heat haze shimmering above the surface of the main road.

By next Monday's visit she would have thought of lots of reasons why someone with the means for such an enviable lifestyle as Max Gold should want to live. She'd bring the subject up with her friends, Maggie and Jane, in the restaurant on Wednesday night. She was going to have a lot to talk about this week.

***

The others in the group were already seated when Anna arrived at Los Dos Caracoles. Smells from the outdoor barbecue awakened her taste buds. As it was summer there was also the smell of holidaymakers. Greasy with sun-oil, they doused themselves in duty-free products to mask fresh perspiration caused by the unaccustomed humidity.

Beside the entrance to the restaurant, a picture of rather unappetising looking snails gave credence to its name. The walls were decorated with lurid paintings of sea creatures and plates heaped with writhing spaghetti topped with splats of reddish-brown.

Squashing in next to Maggie, Anna considered how much to tell the others about Nils and whether to mention Max at all.

Maggie was dark-haired, smartly dressed, slim and capable, married to successful estate agent Javier, with whom she had two sons. She ran a very Spanish household under the auspices of her Spanish mother-in-law. Before her friend had the chance to speak, Maggie put a hand on her arm.

'Anna, have you heard? Max Gold fell from his terrace sometime in the night. He was reported dead on the lunchtime news.'

Anna stiffened as she tried to disguise the impact of Maggie's words. Her outstretched hand faltered as she reached for her wine and the glass tipped, teetered then dropped, shattering on the tiled floor under the restaurant table. Now Maggie was tapping her arm.

'Are you listening? Did you hear what I said? Mind that wine!'

Anna bought time by leaning backwards to co-operate with a quick-thinking waiter who deftly removed breadsticks, olives and aioli before replacing the soiled cloth so swiftly that she might have dreamed the dark red patch which spread alarmingly across the starched table cloth. It would be all right, she just needed time to assimilate Maggie's news and adjust her response. What *was* an appropriate response on hearing one's employer had fallen to his death sometime in the night? Things like that had never happened to her in England. She bent, retrieved the stem of her glass and handed it to the waiter with a mumbled apology.

'Access to the port's been restricted to emergency services. Local police and *Guardia Civil* are swarming all over the place. Weren't you there on Monday?' Maggie's voice was insistent. 'Were they in? Did you notice anything different?'

'Sorry. I did hear what you said. I'm just shocked. It's a terrible shock and I suppose I've lost my job.'

'Oh, I suppose so,' Maggie said. 'Sylvia spoke to someone from the press this afternoon; said she was staying with friends, said she wouldn't go back to the apartment. He used to drink, didn't he? He must have been alone and fallen.'

'Yes, he must have been.'

'Apparently there were no witnesses,' Maggie concluded.

Anna could think of one silent witness to his father's downfall; one with painted eyes that watched and painted lips that would never speak. She shook the image away. She couldn't possibly repeat her conversation with Max now, not even to her best friend. She would be left always wondering whether anything she could have said would have made any difference. Would Max's body still have been lying there when sunrise flooded over this morning's colourful setting of the port?

'I don't mind too much about the work. I hated it really, but I feel terrible about Max . . . oh dear.' The subject needed changing, so after a pause she added 'I'm making progress with my book.'

Anna usually avoided discussing her book, as even for an early draft, her manuscript was full of gaps. But now her dragon had materialised sufficiently to talk about him. In fact he was beginning to feel like a live entity inhabiting her subconscious.

***

Last night in her sleep she had heard his breathing behind her, experienced a sudden chill, a smell like fish, rotting in the sun. She thought she was walking on sand but it became soft downy pillows of fresh

snow through which she began to sink. Then the snow turned into the turned-back duvet with the ringing of the alarm clock.

***

'I've put together my dragon and his cave, now all I need is a castle for the Wicked Queen. Does anyone have a friend with a castle?'

Conversation gradually settled into its usual pattern; talk of families and recent shopping trips. Much of the island's population seemed to be in transit at any given time and who was coming or going or had been sighted somewhere was always a hot topic. Royal family members had been seen having coffee in the port again. Their summer residence, the Marrivent Palace, was nearby.

'Did you actually see him?'

'Who was he with?'

'Was she wearing Prada again?'

'I know where you can buy that outfit!'

'*How much*! You're joking!'

Anna smiled, reflecting how lonely she would have been without her friends and evenings like these. She was the only unattached one in the group and the others were always trying to match-make her with a Jose, a Miguel or an itinerant British businessman. She finished her food, enjoying the banter round the table.

'Hey Anna, how did the Danish pastry for Sunday siesta go down?'

Trust Jane, the grapevine was obviously as well wired as ever; especially considering she'd known Nils less than a week. Jane worked as a reporter for *Meridian*, a publication for English-speaking residents, with offices near the Internet Café.

'His name's Nils and he's a perfect gentleman, thank you very much, so stop trying to make me blush. His home's fascinating and he's taking me out to dinner on Friday night.'

A chorus of 'Ooooh!' circled the table like a Mexican wave.

'Can we come?'

'Where did you meet him?'

'Have you got a photograph?'

'Has he got a brother?'

'As a matter of fact he has. He's a vet in Copenhagen and the last time he visited was three Christmases ago.'

'Do any of us know him? Do you really like him, this Nils?' Maggie asked in a lowered voice, curious about the mysterious Dane.

'Yes. It's a bit early yet, but I think I do,' said Anna. 'He's older than me but he's quite attractive . . . in a way.'

Around the table, speculation started up again.

'Did you stay the night?' Jane wanted to know.

'No, I didn't.'

'Well, we want all the sordid details when you do.'

Jane, from an old farming family background somewhere in middle England, shared an apartment with her female partner, Zhu. Zhu, who didn't join them on these nights out, looked to be of Asian or Oriental ancestry. Her long black hair and sallow skin contrasted vividly with Jane's auburn boyish cut and tendency to freckles. She worked as a therapist in a practice on the ground floor of a large hotel.

'What does Nils do for a living?' asked Maggie.

'He was a farmer in Denmark, somewhere called Jutland, near a town called Viborg or something.' Anna secretly resolved to look at a map.

'What's a Danish farmer doing here?'

'He owns a restaurant. That's where he's taking me this Friday. It's called Mange Tak, it's Danish. It's in San Augustin, have you been?'

Maggie shook her head. 'No, but do you want to meet and shop together one day next week, then you can tell me all about it?'

'All right,' Anna nodded. 'I've still got my ironing job at Red's on Wednesday morning. Let's meet in Dali's about 1p.m. Won't Javier mind?'

'No, he's due a few days' holiday. He's taking both boys to stay with his mother.' Maggie pulled a face.

'There may not be much to tell.'

'Oh, I think there will be,' said Maggie. 'Will you manage okay without the Golds?'

'Well I've only Red's ironing now.' Anna gave a tight smile, 'but I could do with concentrating more on writing.'

Anna knew Maggie was a little disapproving of her association with Red. Ex-public school and vaguely disgraced in some way, he was known by an abbreviation of his surname, Redmayne. Always recognisable, he was in the habit of wearing a battered straw hat, wound around with an old school tie in place of a petersham band. He dabbled in property sales and hired out the two small motorboats he owned. He had a bad habit of casually name-dropping various celebrities who owned holiday hideaways on the island. Lots of people knew who he was, without really knowing him.

'Shall we share a taxi?' said Maggie, waving goodbye to the others still seated round the table.

The party broke up and the two friends headed for the cab rank together. The air was balmy and the hedges atop garden walls released the scent of dama de la noche, night flowering jasmine.

'Don't think about Max and I'll try to get you some more ironing or something to help tide you over.'

Maggie's parting words were good advice, but Anna stayed up late and thought about Max and Sylvia, then she went to bed and thought about Nils. Eventually she fell asleep and drifted into the story coming to life inside her laptop.

***

From the castles highest tower, the Wicked Queen surveyed the land by starlight. All she could see was hers, now she was married to the King.

The Kingdom stretched beyond the Emerald Forest and the Luminous Lake, through the Terribly Tangled Woods and on to the snow-capped Mystical Mountains. Because of an ancient curse, the whole realm was covered, day and night, by the Star-Spangled Indigo Sky. The sky was beautiful but all the people wished the stars would go out and let them see the sun again.

The Wicked Queen had a plan. She was

plotting to get rid of the weak King and have total power, but she also had to deal with the King's young son, Prince Jasper, whom the people loved very much. The Prince's best friend, the dragon called Trog, was by his side most of the time.

Trog never invited visitors to his hidden cave in the snow covered mountains because he had treasure and secrets there. The entrance to his cave was high up and the light from the stars shone like fairy lights on the walls. He lived on small branches and berries and biscuits, from the store in his cupboard of interesting things beginning with 'B'. He practised breathing fire every night when starlight twinkled across the snow and the people were asleep. Without the sun, they still had clocks to tell the time by.

One day, while the Prince and Trog were out building a den in the Emerald Forest, the Queen crept up behind the King and pushed him from the top of the tower. He fell to the ground and was dead.

CHAPTER 4
THE LOVERS

An aroma of fresh baking floated in through the open French windows as city streets stirred into life below.

Nils woke, stretched and lay still, his mind drifting backwards into the past. Backwards across a landscape roughly sectioned by miles of hedges, dry stone walls and small dykes. A landscape where storks nested each year on the thatched roof of his parent's farmhouse, where pink roses climbed the walls. A landscape where pollarded willows and poplars sloped away from bracing west winds: West Jutland was known for its feel-good factor.

In their youth, he and his younger brother Erik would cycle for miles over heathered scrubland, following the tracks of red deer into covered lee of beech and pine. They would return home late in the day, bike baskets filled with wild ligon-berries, mushrooms and herbs to present to their mother. They helped their father tend the family's small herd of Red Danish dairy cows.

The boys' proud parents supported both sons to attend the Royal Veterinary and Agricultural University in Copenhagen; Nils to study agriculture and Erik, veterinary practice. After three years of traveling backwards and forwards to the city, Nils returned to work on the farm, to a remote and solitary world; a world where exactly what happened on farms was comprehended only by the gradually shrinking farming community. Erik studied for five and a half years to become a veterinarian, later establishing a practice in the city. He never returned home from Copenhagen to the thatched farmhouse, except to attend the funerals of each of his parents.

Meanwhile, Nils sought a bride to be a farmer's wife. Young and sturdy, from German stock in South Jutland, Magda was familiar with the rigours of farm labour. Nils knew her family were relieved their fifth daughter had married well, to an educated man they perceived as having property and prospects. So many female progeny and only one son had been a worry. He also knew they understood that farming routines left little time for socialising, and by the time contact with Magda petered out, her parents felt recompensed by her assured future and were anyway already preoccupied with seven grandchildren and two more on the way.

Nils felt slowly burning anger and resentment when Magda proved slovenly in his eyes, and worse, unable to bear children, thereby cheating him out of the future farmhands and heirs he had anticipated. When his patience was tested to the limit, he ended the arrangement with Magda, hired only seasonal labourers and worked alone to reduce the Red Danish herd, slowly turning the arable land over to cereal crops, root vegetables and fruit.

That previous life was now a distant memory under the warmth of the Mediterranean sun.

Looking forward to this evening with Anna made him feel alive again in the old way. With no time for sentiment, he had already decided Anna would be his next companion and partner.

He rose and consulted the large Florentine mirror, seeking some reflection of his youth. The mirror's tarnished backing had curdled to tiny florets of gold around its edges, deifying his six foot, broad-shouldered frame. He saw square-jawed Nordic features, complemented by a carefully trimmed beard. He was confident of his ability to charm.

Outside on the terrace, Tosca watched sparrows checking the old tiles for crumbs, while a strangely composed, excitable little mongrel began making his way down through the precarious detritus of abandoned structures above. Puccini was hoping for some breakfast.

***

'Good evening my friend! How do we do?'

Nils arrived early at Mange Tak and greeted his business partner Holger Trautman as he was placing the evening's menus on crisp white tablecloths. The barman, Angel, was Spanish and the restaurant's clientele, though largely Scandinavian, were a mix of locals and visitors; an understanding that English should be commonly spoken prevailed.

Supplied with records of the week's takings and a large brandy from behind the bar, Nils occupied a table by the open door which afforded a view of the street, where his small red Fiat was parked.

'I shall have company tonight Holger.'

Holger raised his eyebrows. 'Ah-ha, this is a lady, yes? The first we have heard of since Fru Christiansen.'

Nils lowered his head and regarded his associate over the top of his reading glasses. Holger was referring to Eva, the wife he had first met a few years earlier amongst the Scandinavian community here in San Augustin.

‘Mind your business Holger. You know there are things of which I will not speak.’

Holger raised his palms in surrender and went back to the kitchen. He had known Eva well, had been a witness at her marriage to Nils, but she had not been seen for a long time.

Nils was well aware that various rumours circulated amongst the community, but trusted Holger not to anger him by gossiping. Nils himself never mentioned Eva’s name.

It had been agreed that tonight Anna would use public transport as the bus service, although a little erratic, ran practically door to door.

When she arrived at the restaurant, Nils introduced her to Holger then ushered her to a table, suggesting that he order for both of them as Anna studied her menu with bewilderment. A young blonde woman, the wife of the commis chef, politely took the order.

Their meal began with Stinging Nettle Soup garnished with sliced boiled eggs and croutons.

‘To be honest, I didn’t like the sound of this,’ Anna admitted, ‘but it’s delicious.’

‘Nettles are good for bones and skin but must be cooked correctly to eliminate poisons and preserve vitamins. Nutrition of the body is a serious subject. Food has the potential to heal or harm.’ Nils’ smile spread across the lower half of his face, not quite reaching his eyes. Anna put down her spoon and took a gulp of wine.

The rabbit stew which followed was accompanied by a plate of salad and spelt bread.

'We had a school rabbit. I don't think I've ever eaten it before.' Anna studied her plate.

'Ah, a dish equally popular with Scandinavian and Spanish diners; something you must try.'

Following the stew, a refreshing raspberry lime sorbet completed the meal. By the time coffee and liqueurs were served, an intimate atmosphere had developed around the corner table where Nils and Anna faced each other, separated by a flickering candle flame.

'Do you actually work in the restaurant?' Anna asked. 'I'm picturing you with a long starched apron tied around your middle over that blue and white checked shirt. You'd have a white napkin folded over one forearm; or perhaps you wear a chef's hat and brandish cooking implements at everyone.'

'Please feel free to imagine me in whatever scenario pleases you, as long as we two are alone in it so I can cook for you and serve you also,' Nils smiled. 'But no, I made the larger investment some years ago. Now I leave most things to Holger. He is a chef; he has staff in the kitchen. I call in once a week. I help out but I am what I believe you would call a sleeping partner.'

With this last remark his hand, as if accidentally, covered Anna's hand, which she seemed to have allowed, equally accidentally, to remain on the gingham table cloth. Nils gently fingered the gold charm bracelet which Anna wore. He himself wore only a plain gold analogue watch and no other jewellery.

'We should go on for a nightcap, then you must come home for a last coffee. My car is parked outside.'

'But you've been drink . . .' Anna stopped abruptly

as Nils turned his head away. This was not England. She followed him out, both saying adios to Angel, who hailed them from behind the bar.

When returning home from an evening out, Nils sometimes left his car down in a hotel car park on the Paseo Maritimo and climbed three flights of steep, narrow stone steps, wedged out of sight behind a wall at the hotel's rear. These were a little known and rarely used route to the alleyways of Terreno above and also gave access halfway up to Nils' terrace. He made a suggestion that they call into a small Spanish bar near the foot of the steps and fortify themselves for the climb.

The bar's proprietor welcomed Nils, who was well known to him. He had already served two people who were not regulars. Nils saw them immediately, huddled in a corner, whispering beneath the clamour all around.

An overdressed and bejewelled Sylvia Gold looked out of place, draped around a swarthy man half her age. They had been engrossed in each other's company until Sylvia looked up and spotted the newcomers.

Nils knitted his brows. He had never liked the woman. Taking little interest in local news, he was ignorant of her husband's recent fate, the week's frenzied activity in the port and the hastily arranged funeral, necessary in Spain. Neither was he aware of local speculation concerning the couple's relationship, nor the fact that Anna had been employed by them.

Now his attention was caught by Sylvia's startled reaction on seeing not him, but Anna. Her posture stiffened and alarm flooded the over made-up features, adding an even deeper hue to an alcohol fuelled flush. The Saturday night throng around the cramped bar heaved and rearranged itself like a flock of brightly feathered twittering birds trying to land, and when Nils looked again, someone else was seated in the corner. The newcomers pushed away half-finished drinks and tapas which the previous occupants had left behind.

Nils reflected on the puzzling behaviour of a woman he had always thought of as having too much money and too few morals.

'Do you know Sylvia Gold?' The question was abrupt.

Anna, taken aback by his tone, looked up at him. She didn't appear to have noticed the gaudily dressed drinker and her companion.

'Well, actually I was doing some housekeeping for them. Why, do you know them? Did you attend his funeral?'

'So now he is dead.' Nils delivered this statement with narrowed eyes and an air of deliberate disinterest which discouraged further comment. Anna didn't reply.

After a moment's pause, he turned his attention back to Anna and suggested they finish their drinks and climb the stone stairway. He did not wish to spoil their mood by discussing the Golds, alive or dead. Anna's face registered astonishment when he led her through a back exit and an unlocked loading bay at the rear of the hotel, to be confronted by the steps.

'No wonder you don't get many visitors. It's a choice between that narrow alleyway full of rubbish down from the top, or these steps up from below. Aren't they a bit dangerous after a drink?'

'I will take very good care of you. You will quickly agree it is so. I have lived here a long time now.' Nils kissed her on the mouth, slowly but hard, and felt her body soften against his. He took her hand and led the way.

The terrace, when they reached it, was lit by a full June moon; the 'lovers' moon' of folklore. It washed the walls of the terrace with a soft rose burnish. Late night air clung to bare skin. Tosca materialised and brushed by in a silent stroke, then disappeared into darkness. Puccini, the little dog, both ugly and loveable, was nowhere to be seen.

In a decision Nils had already made, although as Anna was to acknowledge later, one she never quite remembered making, he led Anna, who had not sat down and offered no resistance, to the bedroom. The fragile light of fat candles, left lit and sitting in wrought iron sconces here and there, guttered half way up the walls, causing pale gothic shadows to leap on the roughly hewn ceiling.

The time had come, and as if in harmony with this thought, somewhere outside in the darkness, midnight began to strike.

Memories emerged from the shadows and crowded around the big bed; whispering apparitions to be silenced by a new love. Nils wanted to erase the past and share his future with this English woman he had found.

Nils' wife, Eva, had never liked the shadows inside the cave-house. She claimed something there made her fearful. Besides, she was an artist and needed the light to be right. She hadn't liked candles or opera and she hadn't liked cats or dogs named after operas. Nils knew she had believed she could coax him down from his gloomy eyrie and into the city lights but he had proved her wrong. So she rented a small double-glazed apartment in Palma which gradually became her artist's studio. Spending increasing amounts of time there, Eva entertained her own friends some of whom, Nils was reliably informed, were single gentlemen. Unfortunately for Nils, as well as falling in love with the cave-house he was also in love with his wife. He thought of her now with a bitter heart.

Like Eva, Anna was also younger than him, unencumbered by family ties and with a mind of her own. He found her attractive and was prepared to take a gamble on not tiring too quickly of her company. He considered the English to be rather easy-going and fairly predictable, easily embarrassed and quick to apologise. He knew Anna had plenty of friends here, but it seemed obvious that she needed a man in her life, while he needed a woman in his. He had planned their first proper date together to be a memorable occasion and was pleased with his achievement.

When Anna, dwarfed within the giant bed, asked if he might possibly have any English tea, he silently congratulated himself on his foresight during the previous day's shopping trip and disappeared into the kitchen to boil fresh water. Tosca sat soundlessly beside him.

'Ah Tosca,' he said in a low voice, 'now I have *two* beautiful ladies. I think we will keep them both, yes? One day we will show Anna and she will understand.'

Then in a voice raised to carry to the bedroom: 'You have beautiful breasts,' and after a moment, 'do you like milk and sugar?'

Anna struggled into a sitting position, dragging the bedcovers with her, as Nils reappeared in the bedroom's curtained aperture. 'Just milk, thank you. What time is it?'

'Here is your tea and you must stay. You will have no need of a taxi.'

He was completely at ease with his nakedness and moved comfortably between kitchen and bedroom, before sitting on the edge of the high bed and regarding Anna intently. A pathway had been trodden tonight, a bridge crossed, and they would never again be able to meet for coffee with simply a formal 'Good morning' in greeting.

'What are you thinking?' Nils was trying to read her mind. As a boy he had craved raven knowledge, a second sight brought to the Norse God Odin by his two ravens Huginn and Muninn, thought and memory. He had read stories of these dark 'wolf birds' which flew about the world and returned each day to their master with their news and tales of faraway. Nils had always loved to study people and use his silent observations to surprise, manipulate or confound those in his path. He guarded his knowledge and his secrets, storing them carefully.

He was currently considering just when and how to persuade Anna to live with him. He must first establish exactly where and how she lived now, and then begin the task of making *his* home seem preferable. He imagined this could not be too difficult as she was clearly fascinated by the cave-house and, he flattered himself, attracted to its owner. He would be her lover, friend and mentor.

'This tea tastes good. Where do you buy it?'

'Nearby. There is a supermarket which caters for some international tastes. There are Danish dairy products and English tea.'

Nils rearranged the bed cover and settled in beside his guest. It all felt so right. Only one thing had bothered him slightly, but that had been resolved. On her previous visit, when Anna enquired about the store-room beyond the bathroom, she had probably opened the door and it would be some time before their relationship was established enough to hold that particular conversation. The door was now locked, the key safely hidden and meanwhile . . . bats could live in limestone caves.

In their youth, he and Erik had watched the myriads of bats which flitted through the dusk across Jutland in early spring and the summer months. He knew they inhabited the limestone mines at Daugbjerg and Monsted, where they bred and hibernated. Surely there was not a woman who was not afraid of bats.

Later, Nils served more tea as the sun's early rays illuminated the terrace, shining through the first chamber, glancing off facets of the uneven walls and highlighting them like pale hidden gems. He smiled a satisfied smile.

***

The Dragon also smiled. He was familiar with bats; leathery creatures that flew in half-light and slumbered in sheltered darkness. He too knew where they could be found in their gloomy caverns.

He encountered all the creatures of the night as they curiously sniffed the evening air, waiting to emerge. Airborne species made way for him to pass by, alerted by a primeval sixth sense.

He first came many lifetimes ago, after the ice age, towards the end of the sixth millennium BC; He was called from Niflhel, the world of ice and mists and the home of the undistinguished dead. He came as the growth of agricultural communities led to an escalation in the scale of human violence.

He gained entry to Earth's atmosphere in the northern hemisphere as solar winds collided, buckling the energy of the magnetic field into a multi-coloured show of great waves of radiance, and made his home in lands of pagan tradition where people longed for an end to the Arctic night.

He streaked through history, always returning to the human present. He tracked the paths of tides and waterways, the courses of rivers and prehistoric ley lines, through ancient battlefields and the resting places of human dead.

In the eighth century, he followed the sharp keels of Viking long ships as they sliced through the water carrying traders and warriors. He watched as Norsemen, tanned and wild, invaded neighbouring lands, and Canute was crowned king of Denmark and Britain.

He had explored Viking routes from the open borderlands of Jutland around Western Europe and beyond his territory, past Italy and Greece, all the way to Constantinople, just grazing the tip of Mallorca.

For more than half a century now, this route had been overlaid by the only partially demolished Atlantic Wall of the Furher's Third Reich. Coastal bunkers and concrete pill-boxes stood guard from the northernmost tip of Norway all the way to the island known to the ancients as the 'Island of the Pines'.

The Dragon had observed Adolf Hitler's aura with great interest, approving his eventual fate.

CHAPTER 5
THE OGRE

Spike the iguana stirred in the sunshine, listening with his head on one side. In daylight he sunned his leathery hide on the balcony, sleeping inside Red's apartment at night. Folds of loose skin beneath his chin lent him an ancient wisdom, like the beard of a wizened mandarin, but his slothful movements belied the alertness in his yellow reptilian eyes. When exploring, Spike paused to hold things carefully and thoughtfully with slender anthropoid fingers. His diet was a mystery to Anna but she knew there were Tupperware containers inside Red's fridge, and elsewhere in the apartment, the contents of which were best left undisturbed. Now Spike heard her key in the lock. No one else came here besides Red.

Each Wednesday morning, Anna let herself in to mop the tiled floors, dust, wash and iron. Afterwards, if no bus was due, she sometimes sat outside with Spike. She had grown used to his company. Red's balcony overlooked a leafy back road in San Augustin. It was spacious and partially shaded, perfect for penning a few extra paragraphs or a sketch to add to her growing manuscript.

Today Anna went through her usual routine of ascertaining Spike's whereabouts, filling the washing machine and putting the coffee pot on the stove. She opened all the windows, then checked Red's untidy desk for an envelope containing her earnings for the previous week. It was there on top of some half-opened post and a half-eaten baguette.

Sometimes there would be a note with instructions if he wasn't around, which was often. Today's note said; *Hope to catch you before you leave--have something to tell you. Red.*

Anna threw the baguette in the kitchen bin.

'What does he have to tell me, Spike?'

Spike looked as if he probably knew something but wasn't giving anything away. Anna puzzled while she mopped the floor, then decided all she could do was wait for an explanation while she tackled the pile of ironing.

Her first encounter with Red had been in the second-hand English book shop in San Augustin. As the only two customers, they had acknowledged each other by commenting, in a typically English fashion, on the heat. Anna picked up a book of 3D optical illusions and offered a double page spread to Red to see if he could make out the picture. He stared blankly at her for a few moments before speaking.

'Sorry to disappoint you but I've only got one eye.'

He went on to explain he wore a glass eye in the empty socket behind tinted glasses. Anna was horrified by her gaffe. Overcome with embarrassment she agreed to have a conciliatory drink with him in the cramped tapas bar next door, where cured hams hung from their curved hooks like giant slumbering bats. Nauseated by the warm greasy smell, she had cautiously sipped the yellowy-green Hierbas liqueur Red placed in front of her. Why did this sort of thing happen to her?

On learning they had mutual acquaintances and that

Anna could use some paid work such as ironing, Red had entrusted her with a key to his apartment so she could pay a weekly visit.

Anna found having met Red, just as she was dreaming up her one-eyed Ogre, too inspirational to miss; he quickly became the model for a character in her story.

Now, as she folded the last sheet she checked the clock. Maggie would be waiting for her in Dali's at 1pm, which meant leaving Red's early, 12.30pm at the latest. She splashed water over her face, dried her hands and ran her fingers through her hair. Just as she was about to leave, Red entered the apartment, his substantial frame filling the kitchen doorway.

Anna's senses took in mingled odours; sweat and aftershave, lightly laced with alcohol, and a residue of garlic when he spoke. These complemented a faint but ever present petrol smell which lingered on Red's laundry from his boats, the *Red Herring* and the *Jolly Good Roger*. Their owner possessed a certain sense of humour, peculiar to the British but an anathema to other nationalities.

'Ah, I've caught you,' he said.

Anna involuntarily stepped back from the path of her Ogre. She actually felt a little intimidated by Red, although she had denied this to both Maggie and Jane, who each pronounced him to be scary.

He placed his drooping straw hat and a length of oily rope on the kitchen work surface and headed for the fridge.

'Been thinking of speaking to you for a while but decided to let sleeping dogs lie and all that. Anyway, what with Max dying, awful business, and Syl' going off with some foreign fellow . . . game girl, didn't see that one coming; thought now might be a good time. Didn't want to stir up the old mud, you know. Anyway, coast's clear now. Is there any coffee on? How are you?'

What on earth is he trying to say, thought Anna.

***

'What on earth was he trying to say?' prompted Maggie, as she gave Anna's story her fullest attention over lunch in Dali's restaurant.

Dali's was named with reference to Salvador, but didn't display his work. Diners were encouraged to doodle their way between courses on white paper tablecloths, using crayons from pots provided beside condiments and toothpicks. A selection of masterpieces was put on display around the walls.

Anna took a breath; 'Well,' she said, moving the Menu del Dia and leaning forward, 'apparently the old apartment block where I live was built by the Golds, years ago when they first came here and guess what, my apartment on top is the one they lived in.'

'No!' said Maggie. 'What a coincidence. Didn't they ever mention it while you worked there?'

'We never talked much,' said Anna. 'I don't think they knew where I lived. It wasn't of any interest to them. But that's not all. Red says the lock-up garage behind the block belongs to my apartment, but for years has gone unnoticed in the deeds. It's probably never been used by anyone apart from the Golds . . . I've certainly never seen anyone round there.'

'What's it got to do with him and why's he telling you now?' Maggie was intrigued.

'Well, Red and Max seem to have been business associates or something in the past. Red wants me to get access to the garage so he can see what's inside it, now that Max is dead.'

'What a cheek!' Maggie said indignantly. 'Is it locked? Is there a key?'

'That's the trouble. It's bound to be locked and if anyone found an odd spare key somewhere in the Gold's apartment, they'd have no idea what it belonged to. Red thinks I should see a lawyer with my deeds and get permission to force open the door.'

'Wow, how interesting.' Maggie fell silent as they each sipped their drinks and considered the implications of Anna's news.

'What happens next?' she asked finally.

'I suppose I'll make an appointment to see someone,' said Anna.

'Just don't forget to ring me afterwards.' Maggie said. 'And speaking of seeing someone, how did the other night's date go? Are we into earth moving territory?'

Anna recalled Friday evening; the memory of making love with Nils gave her a tingle of excitement. Their lingering parting had lasted well into Saturday, leaving little room for doubt that they were going to see much more of each other. Now she could barely wait for this Friday's planned meeting at the Internet Café. Her mind was playing tricks, asking what if he isn't there? But Nils had made his intentions towards her fairly plain and gave every appearance of being a man who knew his own mind.

'Yes, actually quite high on the Richter scale since

you ask.' She grinned. 'Don't worry, he makes me feel really safe.'

Strong hands had held her while Nils spoke softly into her hair; unintelligible words in what Anna guessed to be his native tongue. She remembered her veins running with quicksilver, melting helplessly into that big bed, enveloped in masculine scents and overcome with emotions. Candlelight flickered in the mirror and everything seemed to be in unstoppable motion. It had definitely been earth moving.

She wanted to return to lie and gaze, from within Nils' arms, beyond the living area out through the tall French windows at new horizons across the bay; warm pastels, red and gold sunsets.

Just then, Jane and Zhu slipped into seats at the next table, each wearing denim jeans and cut-off vests with slogans on them. Jane's was in Latin and Zhu's was in Chinese characters, possibly painted by Zhu herself. Dali's was a favourite haunt of theirs, being close to their apartment on an upper floor of a city centre high rise block.

Jane winked in greeting and began to sketch. Anna glanced at Jane's table cover, which now bore a representation of a Viking helmet with distinctly phallic horns protruding on either side. This was punctured by a painful looking arrow and inscribed, *Anna loves Nils*. Anna gave her friend a withering look.

'Haven't you any important reporting to do?'

'Afternoon off,' Jane said with relish, tipping back her chair.

Anna shook her head. Maggie laughed and Zhu wore her usual expression of a politely surprised smile.

'Might have a bit of local news for you soon,' Maggie said, 'might invite you to a garage opening.'

Anna sent Maggie a warning glance, unsure where this garage business was going and not wanting to anticipate too much. But she needn't have worried; Jane had other things on her mind.

'Anna,' she pleaded, 'can you give me anything at all on the Golds? My editor's chasing me for a story and I can't unearth a thing. Apparently the local police first decided Max didn't fall, he jumped. But Sylvia's completely disappeared so now they've decided he was pushed. You know what they're like.'

Anna knew it was wise to avoid any dealings with the police at all, if possible. She lived not far from her local police station, where young officers lounged outside in a haze of cigarette smoke, handcuffs dangling from their belts, regulation firearms plainly visible.

'Where's Sylvia gone?' she countered. Just how wicked might the Wicked Queen actually be and wasn't this story in danger of becoming too close to her fiction for comfort?

'Word on the street says Morocco,' replied Jane. 'I don't think we'll see her again either. Come on Anna, you must have seen or heard something.'

'I don't know what to say. I'll have to go now, but if I think of anything I'll let you know,' Anna offered lamely. 'I'll ring your mobile.'

Even if Max had been contemplating suicide, it proved nothing, and who knew what went on in Sylvia's head…or for that matter, in her bed?

***

Arriving back at her apartment, Anna sat down in the small living area, a copy of the deeds spread on the table. She had known where to find them; they were inside a cardboard box labelled in her father's hand, FLAT IN MAJORCA. Their dog-eared, yellow folder was randomly embellished with self-important stamps authenticating its contents. Inside, amid more colourful stamps, were details of people involved in successive transfers of the property from one owner to another, recorded entirely in Spanish. Anna guessed her parents, like many before them, had trusted Spanish-speaking English friends to read through relevant documentation when deciding to invest in Spanish property.

She paused at the sight of her father's familiar signature. They would both have been present, he and her mother, planning their retirement together, trying to make a sound investment. Anna's throat constricted; where would she have been? Probably working; you couldn't ever get off school in term-time. She turned the page. Perhaps their choices would lead her down paths her parents could never have foreseen. Aware lock-ups were a rare commodity around the local area, Anna knew they could be a good source of rental income. Towards the back of the sheaf of papers, there was the signature of Max Gold, the first vendor.

Anna checked the word 'garage' in her English / Spanish dictionary. In Spanish it was garaje. Unable to read much Spanish, she began studying each page of the deeds for this word until, somewhere in the middle, there it was.

She picked up her mobile and dialled the number of the Spanish notary who acted as administrator for the block. His answerphone asked her, first in Spanish then in English, to leave her number.

Anna telephoned Benjamin Siegl, an English lawyer she had been introduced to at someone's party last Christmas. He had offered her his card and she had kept it. Ben was able to see Anna two days later on Friday afternoon in his office in Palma.

As she didn't drive, Anna had never taken any interest in the padlocked, grimy-windowed, breeze block garage. It sat quietly occupying its plot in the undergrowth, half-hidden behind starbursts of the pink and white flowers of oleander bushes growing on a neglected strip of land behind the block. Now, perhaps, it was about to be disturbed.

***

Señor Martínez, the administrator, returned Anna's call the following day, expressing ill-disguised irritation and little encouragement regarding the matter of the garage. He nevertheless agreed to spare her a few minutes of his time, although clearly unable to imagine what this English woman could possibly want that wouldn't have kept until the next scheduled community meeting.

As acting Notario who officiated over quarterly meetings for communal matters, Señor Martínez was a man who took himself very seriously. The glisten of perspiration on his forehead and scalp, together with dark patches on the shirt which tightly encased his short stout frame, bore testament to how trying life could be at times. He mopped at his damp forehead with a large damp handkerchief.

He first required Anna to suffer a prolonged wait

behind closed venetian blinds in the humidity of the airless outer office, where sustained contact with the white plastic chair stuck her limp dress to her back and around the tops of her legs. A large oscillating fan droned in one corner and a dusty rubber plant in a tub of caked, cracked earth and surrounded by a halo of spent cigarette butts struggled in another. A wall clock had taken on the stentorian tone of a metronome, timing the young semi-clothed receptionist who flitted in and out of Señor Martínez's inner office with memos.

Kept waiting past her appointed time and in order to fight a losing battle with her eyelids, Anna imagined the memos' contents: Juan says ring him later: Don't forget Maria's day off tomorrow: What time would you like your coffee? God it's hot in here…these plants need some water.

'Señor Martínez will see you now.'

Anna jumped and stood up. The plastic chair re-arranged itself noisily behind her on the tiled floor. In the inner sanctum, Señor Martínez indicated another plastic chair while viewing her suspiciously across his littered desk, the dark patches under his arms spreading slightly.

'How can I help you, Señora?'

'Señorita,' Anna reminded him as she placed her copy of the deeds in front of him.

'How are you, Señor Martínez? Please look at the page I've put a marker in and read the bit I've highlighted.'

El Notario drummed stubby fingernails on Anna's documents while considering the implications of her visit.

It transpired he knew nothing and was unable to

help. The garage, he informed Anna in patient measured tones, had always been there. It belonged to the block. It was locked and no one was interested in it. He doubted its veracity in Anna's deeds and it was not his business to pry into people's affairs. Furthermore, was she a driver? No. Did she have a car? No. Claro. Clearly she had no need of a garage. He advised her to go away and forget about it.

Also, if there was any chance Señor or Señora Gold had continued to use the garage for storage... he wanted to avoid any trouble. He would make some local enquiries then contact Anna if he discovered anything she should know. Otherwise, if he could be of no further assistance he had a great deal of work to do. He handed back the deeds with the air of Hercule Poirot having just solved the latest crime.

As Anna left the office in the base of one of Palma Nova's larger apartment blocks she was conscious of his appraisal of her figure before he dabbed irritably at his brow and switched on his answering machine to listen to his messages.

The outcome was no less than she'd expected, but at least she'd pursued the correct channels. She was happy to wait for her meeting with Ben Siegl and that meant Red would have to be patient too.

In the meantime, her children's story was writing itself inside her head and needed her full attention. She was particularly pleased with her illustrations of the Ogre and his small balding sidekick, Martino.

***

The Ogre had befriended the Wicked Queen

in order to learn her secrets and try to steal her powers. With his cursed appearance, he was feared by most people and was trusted by none.

The dragon Trog was suspicious of the Ogre. He watched the passing seasons from the mouth of his cave.

He was growing older and larger quite fast, and now he could fly as high as the Star Spangled Indigo Sky and breathe fire through his nostrils. However, Prince Jasper was growing up too and the two friends slowly were drifting apart . . .

CHAPTER 6
THE WOODCUTTER

The so-called dry river was a broad empty storm drain. Running the length of the Avinguda Jaume 111, it was designed to carry the flash floods of autumn safely through the centre of the city. Halfway up its steep sides, pink and purple flowering shrubs sprouted through cracks in the concrete, attracting little clusters of butterflies which danced in the sunshine.

Crossing the bridge to the Internet Café, Anna felt nervous butterflies of her own fluttering inside her. Five days without seeing Nils had challenged her confidence in this new relationship. It had been a rollercoaster week of highs and lows. She had stayed away from the café, illogically not wanting to jinx Friday's meeting there.

Now Friday was finally here and Nils was inside, waiting on his customary sofa. As Anna sank down beside him, the familiar light fragrance of his cologne once again evoked an impression of air somewhere other than the middle of the Mediterranean in sweltering summer.

He kissed the corner of her mouth and the soft whiskers of his neatly trimmed goatee aroused sensations which caused a warm flush to start among the butterflies and rise up through her throat, to spread itself across her face and neck. He laid a protective arm lightly around her shoulders.

'You have your laptop. You are writing today?'

'I'll do some later. Or if not, I can do some when I get home. I'll sit outside on the balcony when it cools down a bit.'

A vision of herself seated behind a short line of washing between the folded-up lounger and a large bottle of butane gas reminded Anna of an imminent problem, presented to her that morning ago in an official looking letter from the office of Señor Martínez.

'I've been notified all the power in the block will be off for two or three weeks from next Monday. It's very short notice. I'll have to make some plans to manage without hot water.'

'Really? Most inconvenient.' Nils studied her.

'It's always been unreliable, but it's been getting worse. At the last meeting the community voted to replace some old wiring during the summer. We can manage more easily without power then. It's not a major problem. We all use gas bottles for cooking, but I won't be able to plug anything in, which means no fan and I won't be able to work . . . except here, of course. And my hair might dry a funny shape without a hairdryer.'

Nils looked amused. 'Like you, I too write; articles for agricultural publications, sometimes news journals, but my writing you would find boring I think. However, my terrace is a most satisfactory workspace and my amenities are quite reliable. I have excellent broadband. If you would like to stay with me and use my facilities, you would be most welcome.' He placed a hand over Anna's. 'While you work, if I may, I will bring you coffee and cake.' In a lower voice he said, 'we will also relax when you are not working . . . and your hair is always beautiful.'

Anna adjusted her hair nervously as the waiter placed coffees and Spanish brandies on the table. She wondered how much Nils' proximity might distract her from writing but decided the exercise was worth a try. She did love his unusual home perched high above the bay, she loved coffee and cake . . . and Nils? A little early, but she knew what her emotions were telling her. It was a message she hadn't received for a long time.

'If you don't think I'd be in the way . . . perhaps I could come on Sunday . . . just bring a few things with me,' she suggested, adding hastily, 'it would be really helpful . . . and really nice. Thank you.'

'Wonderful! Come tomorrow, Saturday, for the weekend. We will eat at Mange Tak and on Sunday you can do a little work. My taste in music bothers you, no?'

'Oh no, it's lovely. It's very relaxing.'

Nils gave a wry smile. 'Light opera can be relaxing, yes. It is a world of comedy and tragedy, heights and depths, deep pathos; perhaps you will find it stimulating for your imagination.'

'Yes, I'm sure I shall.' Anna resolved to take opera more seriously in future. Nils had a gramophone player and a collection of vinyl recordings. Perhaps she'd buy some CDs later. She'd heard of Russell Watson and Pavarotti and that group . . . what did they call themselves?

'Well then, we are agreed and I can take you on Monday to collect clothes and other things from your apartment if we still agree.'

Nils left after toasted ham and cheese sandwiches and an hour of cosy chat, saying he had a business meeting in Palma but was impatient for tomorrow.

Anna gravitated upstairs to the mezzanine to work, but found concentration difficult. Eventually she decided she needed something new to wear and deserted the café in the direction of El Corte Ingles, the large department store. Her appointment with Ben Siegl wasn't till four o'clock, which allowed her to shop for a couple of hours.

She arrived at Ben's office with moments to spare, limp with perspiration and shouldering a laptop, but happy that some new lacy, even racy, lingerie made it all worthwhile. Thank goodness they'd had her size; the Spanish were all so petite.

The air conditioning delivered a welcome flow of cooling air as she stepped across the threshold. A concierge, regally suited in aubergine worsted with gold buttons and surrounded by small flickering monitors, waved her beneath potted palm fronds towards the lift doors. Whisked silently from street level and deposited with a soft hiss beside the water cooler, Anna stood on thick carpeting beneath an impressive chandelier in the foyer of suite twelve. The door to the inner office was open. Ben rose to greet her with a welcoming smile and a friendly handshake. He looked cool and reassuring, wearing a lightweight suit, the jacket of which he removed and placed over his chair back.

After a brief assessment of everything Anna had supplied him with, he was able to finally verify her new status as garage owner. He had already consulted a judge in the city and was able to confirm that if Anna's deeds were in order, she could take immediate possession of the garage and, under Spanish law, any contents it might hold. In the absence of a key, he issued her with an official letter giving permission to the police to force entry on her behalf. He sealed their meeting with a final handshake and a request to let him know how she got on.

Anna thanked him, asked that he keep her legal documents, left and caught the bus back to Palma Nova.

The bus route ran past the main city police station, a large and ugly concrete edifice. Anna couldn't imagine visiting either it or its local equivalent over something as insignificant as a locked garage. Also, in spite of Ben's letter, her poor Spanish language skills would make the whole thing embarrassing, but she couldn't deny a mounting curiosity. She considered who among her acquaintances might have a suitably equipped toolbox for the forcing open of locked doors. The one inherited from her father contained aged, rusted implements, most of which she was unable to identify. She had reluctantly thrown them in the basura, the communal rubbish bin.

Nils' apparent dislike of the Golds had discouraged her from admitting any further connection with them. Red had wanted the garage opened, but Anna didn't trust him to share his motives over whatever it was he hoped to find. If controversy arose over any contents, there was always a possibility he remained in touch with Sylvia Gold as he had contacts everywhere; what was that line about letting sleeping dogs lie?

Maggie's husband, Javier, could undoubtedly lay his hands on a drill or crowbar, but Anna didn't know him well. She did know he was always busy and often away from home on business.

As the bus left the city, ascending through the Terreno district, past the entrance to the narrow alleyway leading to Nils' home, Anna thought of the perfect person to help her.

She'd recently introduced a Woodcutter into her story to provide assistance for the Handsome Prince; someone known in the world of storytelling as an enabler or facilitator. The inspiration for his character was based on Eli, a large bear-like man, dark skinned with Arabic features. Probably in his thirties, unmarried and a bit of a loner, he worked in his uncle's delicatessen in a city suburb and lived at the top of the apartment block above the shop. He was also custodian of a luxurious villa owned by an obscure member of the Saudi royal family.

He had been introduced to Anna by an English widow, as someone who could be relied upon for help among the British community, within which he was well known. This applied in any situation whether large and litigious, or small and personal. Eli was a familiar visitor to the clubs and bars around Palma Nova, although strictly teetotal in accordance with his religious beliefs.

Anna had visited the delicatessen and even, one day last summer, been shown around the empty Saudi royal villa; a strange deserted place, where unharvested fruit grew in abundance, only to wither on the branch and the vine. They had walked past trails of melons rotting in the hot sun.

There was an invisible question mark over Eli's existence on the island, something dark but hidden. He was the perfect model for her Woodcutter.

Anna phoned him to see if he could come to help open the garage tomorrow morning. That would resolve the issue before she went to stay with Nils and the electricians began their scheduled work on Monday.

Eli was, as ever, keen to oblige. He moved in different circles to the Golds and held nothing but contempt for Spanish officialdom. He materialised early the next morning with a car boot full of tools, accompanied by his dog Wolfie.

Wolfie was aptly named, being disconcertingly wolf-like. Anna had heard he patrolled the terrace and flat roof area of Eli's apartment block by day and bayed at the moon after dark. He woofed in greeting then, panting in the heat, fixed her in the upturned slant of his pale yellow eyes before settling down, muzzle on forepaws, to watch the proceedings.

Together, Eli and Anna forced apart the flowering oleander bushes; Anna completely forgetting what she had read about the treacherous poison hidden in the tough stalks and how numerous families had lost loved ones, having barbecued their weekend lamb on oleander skewers when no rosemary was available.

She found herself standing on what remained of a rotting Se Vende sign, once erected by a Spanish estate agent whose name she recognised as still being advertised somewhere in Palma; the board was now home to a great many woodlice. The garage door's rusted lock offered little resistance to Eli's drill and he was quickly able to heave it, juddering its grievance, up and over.

The hoops and mallet of a croquet set stood just inside and as the door rose, a small wooden ball rolled towards the intruders, as if from the hand of a playful presence within. Anna and Eli watched wordlessly as it bumped along, coming to rest under the brush of an old lavender shrub halfway down the crazed overgrown driveway. Glancing at each other, they stepped forward into shadow.

An initial scuttering of tiny rodent feet was followed by an expectant silence. It was as if ghosts of the Gold's early lives here raised their heads from a hitherto undisturbed slumber.

Eli's gaze scanned keenly for anything potentially dangerous or valuable. He immediately spotted a decent looking set of golf clubs behind the croquet implements and advanced further. Wolfie sat upright and strained against his leash, which Eli had tied to an exposed tree root. He sniffed the stale air with interest and whined.

In the forefront sat sagging cardboard boxes of what appeared to be kitchen paraphernalia and household junk awaiting disposal; possibly the remnants of a hastily emptied apartment. Beside these, a wicker picnic hamper with loose leather straps and small buckles looked forlorn. Anna bent and carefully lifted the lid to reveal a perfect china tea set boasting a familiar Harrods logo. She recalled the oppressive atmosphere of the Gold's apartment and a small shiver tingled through her, despite the heat of the day.

Plastic balcony furniture reposed under stained chalky seat pads and a burnish of silvery-grey mould. Further in, a candy striped awning with frayed edges sought to trip the unwary with its twisted metal frame. The matching candy striped canvas of folding deck chairs had become a mildewed home for mice and small filmy-white cocoons of something. There was an authentic wooden deck chair which might once have graced a first class deck, cruising an exotic route to faraway places, but whose adventures were sadly over. Beside it lay an extremely dead aspidistra, shrunken roots lying in the remnants of a broken jardinière.

As the eyes of the newcomers gradually adjusted from harsh sunlight to dusty gloom, they caught the glint of a heavy brass ships compass, pointing to the back wall of the garage. Here, beyond a deflated brown canvass dinghy with one oar, utility metal shelving rose to the roof, bowed under the weight of more cardboard boxes and rusty paint tins. In front of the shelving stood a scorched ironing board and rolled-up carpets supporting each other at drunken angles.

Anna and Eli edged further forward, negotiating a route around sturdy crates filled with bottles of dark liquid which, Anna thought, must have aged nicely if the theatrical film of cobwebs was anything to go by; or perhaps not, as the concrete walls and roof of the garage must have slowly oven-baked its contents over a long period of time.

Eli's expression of curiosity was gradually replaced by one of disappointment. This lock-up had revealed no treasures. He oiled the door hinges so Anna could close it herself and arranged, on his mobile, for a locksmith friend to stop by and renew the lock as a favour to him. That done, he was anxious be on his way; an appointment elsewhere beckoned. Also, Wolfie had become restless and was beginning to bark at nothing in particular.

Anna thanked him and said goodbye. Now the garage ghosts had fled, she too acknowledged a tiny bit of disappointment that the lock-up apparently contained nothing interesting or valuable, but the building was itself a very small step up the property ladder. She decided to spend another hour or so checking the boxes and assorted paraphernalia on the shelves.

A shabby, brown leather suitcase, inscribed M.L.G.

in faded gilt, contained an old pair of tennis shoes and a small tin of 'Fisherman's Friend' lozenges. Anna thought sadly of Max. She could never know who he had been, only who he had become. Beside the suitcase was a sharkskin ladies portmanteau, complete with scaled-down cosmetic jars and bottles fitted neatly into the lid. Had this belonged to Sylvia or some older relative? Perhaps it had cruised with the deck chair. Other odd items were broken, discarded, or unidentifiable.

On a lower shelf a couple of wooden crates contained old household tools. Sagging cardboard boxes were filled with an assortment of books, paperwork and untidy files, as if someone had emptied a giant, overflowing in-tray into them. A fat spider hurried on its way while ants went about their business in an orderly fashion. Perhaps a box containing back copies of *Meridian* might be of some interest to Jane. Unsure whether *Meridian* possessed modern micro-fiche technology, Anna resolved to salvage them for her.

She sat for a while on an upturned crate, then decided to have the garage contents removed to the local collection point for rubbish. She would save the magazines for Jane and pass the boxes of papers to Ben Siegl. They must be where Red's interest lay, but she wanted her own curiosity satisfied first.

If Nils brought her to collect things on Monday, perhaps they could leave the magazines and papers in his car boot for delivery. As she had nothing that required storage, she could rent out the garage to one of her neighbours or even consider selling it to boost her flagging bank balance.

Eventually, Anna heaved the garage door down as far

as it would go and went back up to her apartment. Before she packed an overnight bag for her stay with Nils, she planned to spend a few hours working on her laptop.

Her dragon, Trog, had evolved a little differently to her original ideas for him. He of the unmade bed and large cupboard of interesting treasures beginning with the letter 'B' had grown up and was becoming more unpredictable with each chapter. Anna was a little uncertain where all this would end.

***

Trog was spending more time in his cave in the Mystical Mountains, from where his roars thundered around the valleys and his fiery breath flashed like bolts of lightning.

The Handsome Prince Jasper needed Trog's help with some magic, but first he went in search of The Woodcutter. He needed The Woodcutter's help to find a way through The Terribly Tangled Woods to Trog's lair.

***

Trying to concentrate, Anna dozed off in the midday sun.

***

The Norse Dragon entered her dreams again. He stared her in the face, steely, gimlet eyes glinting, penetrating her thoughts. One sharp tusk-like tooth upturned at each side of his mouth framed a malefic grin. Long tendrils writhed beneath his chin like a living beard. He brought with him an aura of freezing cold, as if the weather where he lived still surrounded him, his breath visible, exhaled through wide slanted

nostrils. Wan light caught a slight iridescent sheen on his grey skin like a slick of oil or the damp scales of a fish on a slab.

Menacing in close up, now he drew further away. He was hunched at the back of the empty garage's dim interior. Anna could sense his chill, wintry breath in the darkness. He turned his reptilian head to look slyly over his shoulder and she saw he was fiddling with an old fuse box, which swung open, setting off alarm bells.

***

Anna jerked upright on the lounger, shivering in the heat, her heart thudding, and realised that somewhere inside the building, a phone was ringing.

CHAPTER 7
THE HANDSOME PRINCE

While his guest showered and dressed, Nils had left the cave-house and returned from the streets above with the Mallorcan speciality of thick, spiral ensimadas lightly dusted with icing sugar, and still-warm freshly baked bread rolls. He'd set them down on the table outside, next to a bowl of yoghurt, a plate of figs, pots of conserves, and slices of his favourite Danish Havarti cheese; there was silver-foiled Danish butter, which appeared at most mealtimes.

Currents of morning air carried an aroma of freshly ground coffee across the pages of the Sunday paper he had placed beside Anna. The weathered paving stones under her feet were already warm and the bay sparkled brightly in every direction, filling her field of vision and creating a kaleidoscope of light behind her half-closed eyelids.

She shielded her eyes and watched Nils set the table, wondering whether the traditional calorific British breakfast of bacon and eggs deserved such bad press. Then she buttered a roll and helped herself.

Puccini lay at her feet, sensing she was not someone who would find him a nuisance, and in fact was someone who might even feed him bits of bread and cheese. Tosca sat on the terrace's parapet between its crumbling castellations, washing her whiskers with concentration and feline composure.

'So, I am the handsome prince in your story. Yes?' Nils asked what he believed to be a rhetorical question and carried on talking without waiting for a reply.

Just as well, thought Anna, as the answer would have been *no*, but they could talk about who that character was based on later. Today she would have to tell Nils about Red's revelations and her ownership of a garage if she expected him to pick up and deliver large dusty boxes along with her personal belongings.

'Are you religious, Anna? Are you a Christian?'

'I don't think I'm really sure.' The question was unexpected.

'Do you revere the Madonna and child?'

Anna hesitated. 'I have respect for them. Why, is it important to you? Are you a Christian?'

Religion was something they'd never discussed, and a subject she rarely considered. Allegiance to one or another had been considered to be no more than an accident of paternity, accepted as a fact of life. As a child it had meant long periods of standing reciting things she didn't understand in a cold draughty church. Had she given the wrong answer?

Nils studied her silently, then dropped his gaze, saying; 'Danes have been Christians for over one thousand years. Their conversion from pagan beliefs and pagan gods was a successful political move ordered by Harald Bluetooth. It marked the end of the Viking age. There is an important monument, the Jelling Monument, at Tamdrup church not far from my home in Jutland.'

He unfolded a Danish newspaper and Anna finished the last bread roll, not quite knowing how to respond and thinking perhaps his choice of subject had something to do with the fact that today was Sunday. She wondered about all the things he hadn't told her, might never tell her; things she might or might not find out for herself someday.

Nils was different to anyone she'd previously attempted a relationship with; that was if you didn't count Mr Lovatt the headmaster. The two of them were both older than her, quite serious and wore goatee beards. Mr Lovatt however had had a wife who was leaving him and three school-age children. Who was Nils . . . really? Their strong physical attraction to each other, revisited passionately last night, was quite a surprise.

Her girlfriends had expected her to have acquired a Spanish boyfriend by now but the most likely candidates had all been rejected as being either the dark brooding type, controlling and macho, or emotionally immature Lotharios. Latin lovers, she had discovered, became increasingly less romantic after the first stages of the relationship, when the red roses had wilted on the bedside table and you were arguing over the shopping.

It was difficult to imagine not knowing Nils now; and a more romantic location than this cave-house and terrace with its spectacular view was also difficult to imagine. Hopefully she and Nils would discover how much they had in common, but Nils probably had a lot of chequered baggage stowed in life's left-luggage locker. This would need to be opened very carefully.

She decided to tackle the subject of the garage.

'The other day, someone advised me to check my deeds, because I hadn't known I owned a garage as well as an apartment. It's filled mostly with the previous owners' rubbish but I wondered if tomorrow we could bring some boxes into Palma in the car.'

'Certainly, but who is this someone who knows so much?'

'He's called Red.'

Nils put down his newspaper and removed his reading glasses. 'The Englishman, Mike Redmayne? I did not think you would have such friends.'

'He's not exactly a friend, more of an employer. Why, what's the matter with him?'

Nils gazed into the distance as if formulating his reply. When he spoke, his voice had hardened.

'He has only one eye. He cannot drive but has a speedboat.'

'I know. Two boats actually. I think he was in an accident.' Anna was puzzled.

'Do you know why Mike Redmayne does not drive?'

Anna shook her head.

'In England he was drinking more alcohol than anyone understood when he drove his brother, who had not been drinking, and crashed the car. Your Red lost his eye. His brother did not lose an eye, but he is paralysed from the neck down. The father, Colonel Redmayne, paid his lawyers to keep everything out of court and out of the papers. He and his wife moved to a bungalow with special adaptations to care for the handicapped son. They bought your Red his apartment here so he could move away from everything in England and make another start. Still he drinks and endangers the lives of others. He does not earn his living here honestly and he does not visit his family.'

Nils' tone was contemptuous. Anna felt shocked, having known nothing of Red's history. She was also a little defensive; doing his weekly ironing didn't exactly amount to collaboration. He did sound like a bit of an ogre though.

'How do you know all this?'

'Live long enough on this island and you will learn a great many things. But I am sorry, I have upset you. Please do not think of it.' Nils leaned over, took her hand and kissed it. 'You are a bigger property owner. It is good fortune to be celebrated . . . but why has this "Red" as you call him, told you now?'

'Well, the garage was last used by the Golds years ago and now they're not here anymore. I'm hoping you won't mind bringing some boxes of documents and other stuff into Palma. I'm handing them to my solicitor as they're legally mine and I don't know what else to do with them.'

'What are these documents?'

'I don't know. I'm not really interested, but someone should check there's nothing important there before I get rid of them. They're mostly in Spanish.'

Nils studied the middle distance again, his brow furrowed. 'These papers . . . how old are they? There is correspondence?'

'I've no idea how old they are or what they're about. That's really what I want a solicitor to check first, then we'll probably just throw things away. It won't take him long to go through everything; it would take me ages, plus I wouldn't know what I was looking for.'

Nils made no further comment.

***

The little red Fiat was unloved. Dirty and gritty from unmade roads beyond the city; the seat-covers smelled stale from too many journeys made with Puccini unrestrained, bouncing excitedly on the back seat. Today the back seat had been reserved for Anna's suitcases, freeing the boot and roof-rack for boxes.

They pulled into the side street with resident parking for Anna's block. The building looked forlorn. No vehicles were parked in the immediate vicinity. There was no evidence of the other residents or of electricians at work. The flaming profusion of bougainvillea cladding the walls flourished undisturbed.

Entering the building, the stairwell was deserted. Anna checked the mailboxes. All were emptied, leaving a discarded lottery ticket and a sticky lollipop behind. The lollipop was surrounded by a posse of ants. A trail of dropped pistachio shells and the occasional acid green nut descended the stairs and crunched underfoot.

Schools were closed now and Anna realised that Spanish residents had probably been moving out during the week. Different here to school holidays in England; the two month long summer holiday seemed to go on for ever. Families spent it mainly on the beach. Children here seemed so much better behaved, happier.

The notification of work commencing had said 'Monday early' but time on the island often carried little meaning, especially in the summer months. The proposed three weeks could last until autumn. How lucky to have met Nils; without immediate family here, what would she have done? Anna closed her apartment door, causing a hollow sound to echo down the empty staircase.

Back outside the building, around the garage, the flowering oleander shrubbery which she and Eli had trampled just two days earlier had already reasserted itself, closing ranks. Anna thought of the briar hedges in the story of Sleeping Beauty.

She and Nils retrieved the boxes, leaving behind the sad miscellany the garage had guarded for so long, waiting under its layer of dust. Gold dust, Anna thought as she turned the new key, delivered that day, in the new lock.

On the journey back to Palma, she suggested the documents and magazines could be temporarily kept in the store room behind the bathroom. Recently discovering this to be firmly locked had re-ignited her curiosity and she now saw an excuse to explore without seeming to be too nosy. Nils however, preferred to deliver them directly to Ben's office, which did make sense as the boxes were already in the car and the car was on its way to Palma.

Ben was happy to take custody of boxes of old paperwork, assuring Anna he would contact her shortly with a précis of the contents. All that remained in the car boot were the old copies of *Meridian* for Jane, who Anna intended to see later in the week, having extracted a promise that her friend would put nothing in print about the garage or its connection to the Golds. None of it was very newsworthy, but Mallorca was a small island.

That evening, Nils apologised that it was necessary he go to the restaurant to see someone on business.

'You are welcome to accompany me or you may

make yourself at home here. I should be only one hour, maybe two but no more. The occasion is not a social one. I could bring us late dinner when I return.'

'I'll just stay here then, if that's alright. I'm quite tired.' Anna planned to have a relaxing bath. She felt comfortable in her new environment and was becoming used to Nils' gruff and unselfconscious manner.

He showed consideration for her needs and comfort and there was plenty of room for two to live in the cave-house, providing they shared the large bed. That was the best of it. The bedroom was a little cooler than the main living area, being further back into the rock. It was also furnished with a large fan directed at the bed. Of course this did nothing to cool the ardour of new love and Anna's skin felt hot and angry with a surfeit of daytime sun and night-time passion.

After Nils had left for Mange Tak she ran a bath, sinking luxuriously into the balm of her favourite bath oil. She was completely relaxed when she heard a noise. She lay very still in the warm water, listening, and it came again; sounding like a scratching or clawing that made the roots of her hair tingle. Could it be a rat?

Anna wasn't frightened of rats, but like most people she didn't like the idea of being too close to one, especially not in a confined space. Scratch, scratch, and Anna reflected that the bath was an old-fashioned roll-top style which meant something small could run beneath its splayed clawed feet. Whatever had made the noise had her full attention and she sat up very cautiously.

A short silence was followed by more muffled noises and now it was clear it was coming from the other side of the locked wooden door to the store room.

'Puccini?'

Total silence followed; surely Puccini would have barked or huffed and gruffed at the sound of her voice. He would want to be let out.

The silence lengthened until Anna ventured out of the bath. Nervously, she tried the door handle, this time silently praying for it to be locked. It was.

The bathroom was partly aired by a duct positioned high up in the wall with an outlet to the terrace. Otherwise, steam escaped, aided by the large fan, through the bedroom, which had no door, and out through the living area, the French windows of which were usually standing open.

The cave's high ceilings meant this arrangement never felt claustrophobic. Excessive humidity was a problem on the island anyway where, Anna knew, even in the priciest air-conditioned apartments, carelessly stored clothes and bedding soon developed tell-tale stains of mould.

She quickly dried herself in the silence, and then padded into the living area, barefoot, wearing a thin saffron coloured Indian-cotton kaftan smelling faintly of ylang-ylang and patchouli. She had put it away when they went out of fashion more years ago than she cared to remember. She inhaled the garment's lingering scent. It was sufficient to take her back in time and she thought, here I am again, lighting candles, opening wine, only instead of a flat in the north of England I'm in the middle of the Mediterranean twenty years later, I'm a writer and I'm in a relationship with a fantastic man.

Tosca was curled on one of the settees, and when

Anna stepped out through the open French windows she could just make out the shape of Puccini sitting inside the gate at the far end of the terrace, waiting for Nils.

She sat down with her glass of wine, frayed nerves calmed by the familiar lights and sounds of life in the city below. She wondered again what else besides wine was in the storeroom. When he returned, Nils would explain the scratching noise she had heard and put her mind at rest.

Beyond the terrace gate, behind the wall on the other side of the alleyway, rose the top of an iron shaft which housed the mechanism of a lift cage. The lift carried late night revellers from the lobby of a large front-line hotel below, up to a night club sited in its penthouse suite, which was beneath and to the side of Nils' terrace.

On most nights, a frenetic bass beat could be faintly heard resonating in the warm air and the darkness of the lift shaft was illuminated by a cascade of bright neon shapes which tumbled from the top, stacking up like a trove of jewels, to fall away then build and tumble again, over and over until dawn.

City night-light dimmed the stars, but some familiar constellations could still be traced overhead, making Anna think of her Handsome Prince character. She brought her laptop from the living area and opened it on the table.

***

She had first met Jamil when she ventured into his shop to make an enquiry for someone Maggie knew, a client of Javier's estate agency. Jamil would have been very gratified to know that he was the model for Anna's Handsome Prince.

His work, about which he was passionate, was the acquisition, restoration and sale of antique carpets. Always referring to himself as Persian, since the country was still Persia, not Iran, when his parents brought him as a boy to live in Spain, he took great pride in the cultural heritage of his ancestors. These woven works of art left his backstreet workshops to be sold in his shop, silkily resplendent in their stained-glass blues, violets and vermilions. Displayed together with religiously styled artefacts, they chimed with the Moorish design of some of Spain's older architecture, known as Mudéjar. Jamil's clients were mostly wealthy people. Disappointed by his lack of height, he wore expensive hand-crafted shoes with a hidden elevation, dressed for business in western clothes and constantly adjusted his immaculate shirt cuffs. He attended his shop never less than perfectly groomed, exuding the agitated energy of one who is late for something important.

Anna always secretly enjoyed the scent of his cologne, having decided it smelled discrete and very expensive. His breath smelled faintly of something aromatic which she could never place.

***

Prince Jasper sat in the palace surrounded by his magnificent carpets. He wore gold rings on his fingers, one with a royal crest. His white jewelled turban and midnight blue robes complimented his dark handsome features, but his face was sad.

He had become a doer of heroic deeds, worshipped by his people, but his plan to bring back sunshine to the land needed the help of

Trog. Only Trog, his childhood friend, knew which of his carpets had the power to fly. But Trog no longer came to visit him.

So one fine day, the Prince took off his rings and his white jewelled turban, picked up his sword and set out with the Woodcutter, who was big and strong. Together they headed for the Terribly Tangled Woods.

***

The terrace gate grated open and clanged shut. Nils advanced through the shadows bearing a covered tray of food, Puccini trotting behind him.

'It is as I said, no more than two hours and we have here good food.'

He arranged the dishes on the wooden table and brought cutlery and napkins out from the kitchen.

As they ate, Anna told him about the noise she'd heard and asked what he thought might have caused it.

Nils displayed neither surprise nor concern, explaining that some years ago, during the time when the abandoned buildings above were inhabited, gitanos, Spanish gypsies, found a way down through a crevice in the rock. To reassure his wife Eva, he had sealed off their route and never been troubled since, but, more recently, a colony of bats had found their way in and set up home. Undoubtedly it was one of these creatures that had frightened Anna. They were a protected species, of no danger to man and best left undisturbed, which was why he kept the door locked.

Anna couldn't decide which was worse, rats or bats. She was curious though, about the absent Eva and disappointed by Nils' apparent lack of photos, either of himself or family members. She knew of his brother Erik, the vet in far-away Copenhagen, but still knew little of Nils' former life or how he had come to settle in Mallorca.

'Tell me about Eva.'

'My wife was easily frightened. She was frightened of her own shadow. She talked always about the light, the light and the dark. She could not paint if the light was not to her liking. I would prefer to talk of other things.'

'Tell me about farming in Denmark and why you came to live here.'

Nils pushed back his plate and took a long drink from a glass of his favourite Jutland beer, brewed at Sogaards and available in his restaurant.

'I came in the eighties. Farming in Denmark had gone large scale, industrial. Everything was different. Everything was about *krona*, money. In the year of nineteen-eighty, V.A.T. was twenty-two per cent on alcohol and on tobacco and on property. The Government said Danish health would be improved but it was not so. They put a yoke around the necks of farmers and drove us for profit. I grew food for markets and restaurants; vegetables, fruits and many berries. I had cultivated the heather-lands. I was interested in organic, but they wanted only animal feed and Christmas trees for export. I did not care to be a labourer or a pig farmer.'

Anna listened in fascination. It was the first time Nils had really talked about his earlier life. 'What made you choose to come to Mallorca?'

'I had holidayed here, together with Erik; in our youth we cycled around the island. We met a farmer with a goat with a broken leg and made a splint for it. The farmer's wife gave us food and a bed for the night. I had memories of the warm climate, warm people and a simple way of living. In Jutland we also had a big blue sky and a wild green sea and many miles of sand but the small farming communities had lost their way, lost their quality of life. Winters were harsh, with little relief in the summers. Erik was better off in Copenhagen. At the end I came here. I had a small boat; I sailed it around the coastline.'

'Did you sail here all on your own?'

'All Danes have sailing skills, many have boats. Seafaring is in our blood. I met Holger and we joined together in business.'

'Do you go back to visit? I love the countryside.'

Nils slowly shook his head. 'No, but the Danish countryside . . . yes,' he spoke quietly, almost to himself. 'The storks have all gone now; our national bird is the lark since nineteen-sixty. Do you know they say that chaffinches sing in dialect in the beech woods?' He pushed his chair back abruptly, stood up and carried their tray with the remains of supper into the kitchen. The window in time had closed.

Nils remained preoccupied, even in the bedroom, stripping off his clothes and sinking back on the bed without his customary pause before the mirror. In the dark, they made love but Anna could tell that recalling his earlier life had disturbed him. She fell asleep wondering if, after bats in the bathroom and tales of Denmark, she would dream of the Norse Dragon again. However, fate, it seemed, was looking the other way.

***

She floated through a deep hued landscape;

waving fields of tall flower stems and lupines in every shade of purple and pink, gentian and navy delphiniums. Around the edges, huge pink hollyhocks stood tall and stately. The sweet summer air smelled of fruit, cider apples; Anna could taste their tang in her mouth. Long grasses swished softly in a light breeze; the tall flower stems bent towards her.

The scene was backed by dark green head-of-broccoli trees which sheltered a slatted barn, painted red and green, with a chimney stack and a curl of smoke. Orange and lemon wedges of sunshine radiated like the sails of a windmill.

***

On waking suddenly, Anna recalled the designs on collectable chinaware she had coveted back in England, aptly named Bizarre. It all seemed a lifetime ago, when things like that mattered.

CHAPTER 8
THE FRIENDS

At a small aluminium table beneath a weathered awning, two elderly Hispanic men played silently with the communal dominoes, making only a decisive rap noise as each piece was laid. Inside the bar behind them, on an elevated screen, a news-reader babbled excitedly in Spanish.

Nils settled at the other small table, making the feet of the light chair scrape on the gritty pavement while the table rocked, slopping the glass of coffee sitting next to a measure of Spanish brandy. He placed his carrier bag of fresh bread, fruit and ham, bearing the logo of the nearest supermacado, beneath the table and tipped his brandy into his coffee.

He had come up into Terreno to run some errands, leaving Anna writing on the terrace. Alone, his thoughts turned to her recent experience in the bathroom, which had made him wonder whether old problems he had believed resolved might be re-surfacing.

Of course, women were known to have hysterical imaginations; however, Anna would disappoint him greatly if that were so in her case. He had judged her to be stable; an unmarried English school teacher writing stories for children, surely a good choice. He didn't want to have to revise his decision. Besides, he was getting too old to spend time courting the opposite sex. If Anna settled and they remained compatible he was prepared to offer marriage at some time in the future. Later years would seem less daunting if faced with a partner by his side. Extended family were not an issue in this case, he only hoped Anna's friends would not exert an undesirable influence over her.

He had agreed to deliver some old magazines tomorrow evening to the one called Jane and already had misgivings about the encounter. He felt very mistrustful of people driven to seek a partner from amongst those of their own sex. Didn't Anna meet Jane for lunches somewhere called Dali's, and hadn't Dali been a repressed homosexual in love with Federico Garcia Lorca? The more he thought about the subject, the more it bothered him. At the same time he owned a certain curiosity regarding women inclined that way, but surely Anna should choose her friends with more care.

It was true he had left Denmark disillusioned by the economic situation, as he had explained to Anna, but another development of which he disapproved was also disrupting Danish society back then; the rise of the so-called Red Stockings, radical women's collectives emerging everywhere. They complained about men, discrimination and anything else they could think of. They even held island summer camps from which men were banned in order to plan secret campaign strategies. Laws were being changed and everyone talked of equality. Without doubt, the world had gone mad. A man's wife should be his business and no one else's. She should serve her husband and her marriage.

The Spanish had their failings, but at least they

retained some correct values; although even here, he had seen times change dramatically. What remained of the generation liberated after Franco were just the old guard now. This island seemed filled with irreverent new Spanish wealth, students and tourists.

'God morgen, god morgen! Are you alone?' Holger called in greeting as he approached the small bar. 'Your look is most serious.'

Holger visited the wholesalers in Palma on a Tuesday morning and his way back to San Augustin took him through Terreno.

'God morgen, buenos dias. Be seated.'

Nils moved his purchases and Holger eased himself awkwardly into the aluminium chair. He was a large man, due to his professional proclivities and a Spanish wife at home who also loved to cook. A rivulet of perspiration ran from the hollow of his neck into an exposed 'v' of chest hair.

'How is Maria?' Nils was fond of Holger's wife.

'Maria is well. How is Anna? Where is Anna?'

'Anna is well. She stays at my home today while I shop.'

'Ah, she will make a good wife my friend,' said Holger mischievously.

'Hmm, that may be,' replied Nils.

The barman came outside, setting a tall glass of lager down in front of Holger. The glass immediately frosted and Holger drank from it with relish. He and Nils watched wooden crates being unloaded outside a bar across the road. The dominoes behind them were scooped up and clattered noisily into their wooden box.

‘Anna is a nice woman,’ Holger observed.

‘That is so but it is her friends and acquaintances I am concerned over. She did work for Max and Sylvia Gold, whose affairs were always most suspect. She currently works each week for the Englishman, Mike Redmayne. Do you know of him?’

‘He is a real estate agent here. Ja?’

‘If you wish to call him so. He circles the island in his boat, noting luxury villas displaying sale signs; he takes photographs, obtains particulars then advertises privately, undercutting the real agents. He trespasses on private land, taking prospective buyers for viewings of properties standing empty. With no office to run, no business to promote and no overheads, he makes lucrative deals. He approaches the owners directly on behalf of his ‘clients,’ with whom he has meetings in bars all over the island. He name-drops his more wealthy clients most shamelessly.

‘He is a successful man.’ Holger looked impressed.

‘The man is a shark, a troll, an ogre, Holger. I have also observed Anna entering the shop of a wealthy Arab carpet seller whose goods she could not possibly afford to buy. What sort of associate is he?’

‘You must ask Anna such questions, my friend. I cannot answer, but tread with care if you like this woman.’

‘You know me, Holger; I am always careful. Tonight I go with Anna to the apartment of her friends in Palma. I will be most interested to make their acquaintance. However, now I must leave you. I will call at the restaurant later in the week as usual. We will hope business is good. Ja? Skål, my friend.’

'Make sure to enjoy your evening.'

Holger drained his glass and the two men left the table in opposite directions; Holger to climb into the familiar white van with a distinctive logo of an undulating Danish flag, white cross in a red field, with Mange Tak written across it.

***

Nils might have conceded the apartment belonging to Jane and Zhu wasn't what he expected but then, if he was honest, he hadn't known exactly what he did expect.

The living space reflected two distinctly different tastes. It was furnished with dark antique furniture which could have been shipped from England. On the walls, oils on canvas depicted equine thoroughbreds and hunts with hounds. Suggestive perhaps of Jane's background, Nils wondered curiously.

He automatically attributed the watercolours and elegant pen and ink drawings, blossoms, cranes and water-lilies, to the obviously oriental side of Zhu's heritage. However, large printed coloured charts and startlingly graphic medical diagrams tacked up here and there definitely challenged his expectations. Such contrasting styles left him lost for a suitably appreciative comment in Danish, English or any other language.

Anna introduced him to her friends and his hand was shaken, heartily by Jane, delicately by Zhu, who retreated to the kitchen to brew fresh coffee. Jane offered him aquavit, which impressed Nils in spite of himself.

'Thank you, this is much drunk in my homeland.'

'The tap water's okay here in Palma but I prefer the odd glass of this.' Had she winked at him?

'Zhu gets it from the hotel. Sit down and make yourself comfortable.' Jane indicated a large leather-covered chesterfield.

Nils sat down, feeling uncharacteristically self-conscious. He studied a striking poster he thought reminiscent of the repeating patterns of British avant-garde artist Andy Warhol, whose work he had admired in his youth; it was of row upon row of small stoppered bottles filled with varying layers of vividly coloured liquid.

'Aura Soma,' Jane offered cheerfully as she balanced herself on the arm of an upholstered chair, 'Indian healing system; uses colours in diagnosis.'

'Ah, your friend is, I believe, a therapist. What therapy does she practise? In Denmark non-medically qualified people may practise but their activities are restricted by law. They say reflexology is most popular.'

'Oh, Zhu's into auras, especially the astral layer. She does colour therapy and Reiki.'

'What is . . . Reiki?'

'Energy therapy; helps clear an imbalance or blockage so chi, the life force, can flow around the aura. People who have it see fabulous colours; some have said it's like sharing your soul.' Was she mocking him?

'Most interesting; your friend sounds talented but what people want this service? Are they ill or deluded; perhaps they are here on holiday?'

'All sorts; the quick and the dead.' Jane grinned. 'Actually, I think quite a few of Zhu's clients are Scandinavian.'

Nils raised his eyebrows. 'Does she have all the correct documentation to practice?'

'Of course; she trained under a Welsh lady actually, in Britain, Merrijoy Winter, that's when we met.'

At this reminder of his hostess's lifestyle, Nils looked over Jane's regular features, short auburn hair, white short-sleeved shirt, denim jeans, and was reminded of all the questions he wanted to ask; questions which good manners forbade. Instead he made small talk.

'You have a very nice apartment. What exactly do you yourself do; some kind of journalist I believe?'

'Yes, for *Meridian*, have you read it? It's an English publication here. General factotum, reporter, journalist, general dogsbody; journalists never sleep.'

'Hmm . . . I may have seen a copy, some time ago.' Nils raised his hand to rub the back of his neck, his shoulders twitching with a sudden shiver. 'Your air-conditioning system is most efficient.'

'Oh sorry.' Jane jumped up to adjust a wall setting. 'I turned it up before you came. It's so humid tonight, I've closed the balcony doors. Should we go into the kitchen? Anna took the magazines through there and Zhu was making some coffee, or you can have tea, lager or wine.'

Anna and Zhu were seated at a large pine table, where Anna had put down the box of old copies of *Meridian.*

Jane began flicking through them, disturbing their remaining residue of sandy grit and dust clusters. 'I've seen a few of these before but not the older ones; really interesting, thanks Anna.'

The kitchen was high ceilinged. An old fashioned rack designed for airing clothes hung above the table. It bore a number of s-shaped butcher's hooks from which handfuls of drying herbs and the odd kitchen utensil were suspended, together with two brassieres and what might have been half a dozen G-strings; Nils hastily looked down.

He saw the fitted units were a little dated but solid and of good quality. A tall pine dresser stood against one wall, displaying a random collection of china plates, mugs and rustic Mallorcan earthen-ware.

Zhu poured him some coffee from a small pot standing on the hotplate. Her scent was tantalisingly discrete, a hint of something . . . then only the aroma of fresh coffee. Delicately built, her long dark hair tied back from fine features; she moved gracefully and noiselessly. She reminded Nils of Tosca; lithe and sleek.

'You have no pets?' he asked, making conversation.

'There's an aquarium in the bedroom. You can have a look if you like, but the bed might not be made.' Jane cast a fleeting glance towards Zuh, the corners of her mouth twitching into a private smile.

Nils changed position on his chair and ran a forefinger around the back of his shirt neck.

'Are you warm or cold?' Jane asked.

'Oh, I am fine, thank you. I will make a visit to your bathroom if that would be in order, then we must leave soon.'

'Into the passage and first door on the left,' said Anna, looking up from a copy of *Meridian*.

Nils noted with displeasure that she obviously knew her way around this apartment. His discomfort grew and he reminded himself he hoped to distance her from such friends.

He looked into the bathroom mirror, wondering whether any other men had ever looked at their reflections here, and what Jane and Zhu would say and do after their guests had departed. Also he was of the opinion they should have their air-conditioning looked at; women were notoriously careless with such things.

***

The Dragon studied Nils with his head tilted to one side. He had never seen a clear reflection of himself.

He loved colours. He especially loved the northern lights, the way they passed across the heavens in great waving fluorescent streamers. He knew the Vikings believed them to be reflections of the armour of the Valkyrie, the warrior virgins of Norse mythology, while to other human Arctic dwellers they represented the ghosts of long-dead ancestors. To him, the aurora borealis was the thing of the most pure beauty in the universe; the thing that gave him birth on Earth.

He could see the energy of the universe pulsing through everything, slowly with spiritual entities, fast with physical bodies. He could see human auras quite clearly, vibrating and shape shifting around their owners. The third layer or astral plane carried shadows, imprints of the dead. They called out to the living but their voices were rarely heard.

Tonight it was as if proximity to Zhu had aroused this layer in Nils' aura, causing it to vibrate violently.

The dead of course were all around, but humans were not very perceptive creatures; unlike animal species for which the Dragon had respect, but which

were outside his remit, not meriting fate in the same way.

He was entertained by the efforts of certain rural groups of Spanish gypsies who travelled constantly away from their burial grounds to avoid those known as mulos, the spirits of their dead, only to have the mulos trailing wearily behind them from one location to the next.

***

When Nils returned and paused in the kitchen doorway, Anna was telling Jane and Zhu about the garage.

‘Who’s Eli?’

‘What does he do?’

‘Sort of . . . helps with things. He works in his uncle’s delicatessen and as a sort of caretaker of a huge estate in the middle of the island. He brings me surplus fruit and leaves it outside the door if I’m not there; melons, oranges, grapes, figs . . .’

‘I see’, said Jane with exaggerated inflection.

‘No,’ said Anna ‘it’s not like that, it’s something to do with his religion. People accumulate good turns in their lifetime to improve their prospects in the afterlife. They try to give as much as they take. It’s about balance.’

Zhu nodded slowly as if she understood, but Jane remained sceptical.

‘Are you sure he doesn’t buy the fruit to make an impression?’

‘No, he took me to see the estate where everything’s grown.’

'And he's got a friend called Wolfie?'

'No! Wolfie's a dog!'

Nils had heard enough. His concerns over Anna's friendships were multiplying by the hour. Nevertheless, he decided to sit and finish his coffee. Manners were always important, no matter the situation. He adopted a benign expression and listened while the others discussed a scoop Jane was chasing involving a local celebrity, but he couldn't lose the uncomfortable sensation that someone was breathing down the back of his neck. He loosened the second button of his shirt collar and smoothed the knees of his slacks with damp palms.

He considered a conundrum to which he could find no answer. He was sexually attracted to women like Anna, normal feminine women with feminine ways. Of course he had never understood the obsession of such women with their clothes, their hair and use of cosmetic preparations, but assumed it was to please men and therefore must be tolerated by men, and paid for by someone.

But he also admired Jane's clean freckled face and practical haircut. She was clearly an intelligent woman, whose freshly laundered no-nonsense shirt teamed with neat jeans won his approval; quite Danish in fact. He had expected to encounter hostility towards men but Jane was neither hostile nor aggressive, not how he imagined the Red Stockings to be. In fact he found her to be good company; her cheerful personality being what he would have described as gay, once-upon-a-time. Now the conundrum was; knowing her lifestyle, how could she possibly be warranting his approval, and also why did being gay have to imply something so undesirable now?

He had always prided himself on his grasp of English, not least because it was, as everyone said, a difficult language to learn, with a rapid cultural evolution. Either the world around him was speeding up or he was slowing down. It was time to go home.

As he and Anna left the apartment, Jane reminded Anna a table had been booked for their next girls' night out at Caracoles. Zhu said something quietly which Nils couldn't catch and as he headed for where the car was parked, he resolved again to take more control of the social situation. Anna was in need of the right kind of guidance. It was surely her good fortune they had met.

The heat and humidity outside enveloped them like a warm damp towel. The colours were of the city at night, either shadowy or neon bright and even this late, approaching midnight, scantily dressed young people queued everywhere; for fast food, for entry into clubs, for buses, for trains, or window shopped arm in arm.

There were gitanos on street corners, looking for opportunities, or perhaps just looking. Nils disliked them, these urban gypsies with dark darting eyes. The women, with their elaborately oiled and coiled hair, who by day harassed passers-by with buttonholes of supposedly lucky heather; the menfolk, who emerged at night, slim and artful in gaudy waistcoats.

Their presence right in the commercial heart of the city would never be tolerated in Denmark. History recorded that in fifteen-eighty-nine, Denmark had introduced the death penalty for gypsy ringleaders. In fact, Sweden had followed up fifty years later by hanging all male gypsies. Putas, thought Nils; pimps and prostitutes.

They were here because remnants of the old city still lay immediately behind the façade of rapid development spreading outwards from the city's heart. Less than three streets away from the huge new department store stood crumbling tenement blocks. These rabbit warrens with their name plaques gone, barricaded with rubbish, wooden pallets and car parts, created anonymous addresses identifiable only to their vagrant occupants. Doorways were filled with bare-footed children who stared and ran into shadows at the sight of an unknown face; their existence lived beneath the radar of city life, veiled from the uninitiated. Tourists rarely blundered in here and any finding they had done so would hastily seek a way back out.

Nils would have been disturbed to know that Anna would be visiting these tenements before long. But for now his world felt secure and his dreams were untroubled.

In sleep, his subconscious roamed to Viborg, the old town and place of Viking sacrifices, where he once sowed the wild oats of a young man. Mostly he returned to boyhood haunts revisited in adulthood, uncultivated places where he trod secret paths through the beech and pine forests of Jutland, over fallen branches, bare and blanched, covered in a filigree of lichen which clung like small natural sponges, silver, bone coloured and green.

He walked on beaches of pale sand, deposited by glaciers at the end of the last ice age. Here and there, where marram-grass gained purchase, patches of deep waving shadows changed from green to gold as the year turned across the undulating landscape. Sandy pathways between the rustling hillocks lead over tidal flats, where sea lavender hummed with industrious bees. The restless ocean, its surface whipped by the west wind, infiltrated miles of dunes, so the shoreline shifted constantly and no map was ever accurate.

Together with Erik, he went bird spotting on hinterlands composed of salt marsh and reed beds, and on long expeditions to gather seaweed for thatch and fertiliser. This was a happy history, that Eva had spoiled for ever.

As images of his wife infiltrated his dreams Nils woke and remembered how much he hated her.

CHAPTER 9
A MYSTERY

Anna's Wednesday mornings were still reserved for Red's ironing. Nils always made his disapproval of the arrangement very clear.

At breakfast he had, at Anna's request, translated the title of his current piece of work as *Chaotic and Regulatory Death among North Sea Species*, explaining it concerned fish stocks in the North Sea and he would be busy all day. Anna had wisely decided not to pretend too much interest.

To her relief, Red had been absent from his apartment, so conversations concerning the garage were avoided, but Anna had returned to the cave house with something else on her mind.

After leaving Red's, she'd paid a visit to Ben's office in Palma. The suited concierge had informed Ben's office of her arrival and waved her in the direction of the lift.

Ben had prepared a précis of the contents of the files of old paperwork and, as anticipated, it listed mainly copies of long-ago transactions, old details of properties long since haggled over and sold, queries, replies, orders and invoices; faded carbon copies bearing smudged details and illegible signatures. Nothing of interest or worth keeping emerged apart from some curious personal correspondence found in the most recent file. It referred to a piece of real estate situated on Palma's harbour front. Ben showed it to Anna.

'Isn't this near where you live?'

Apparently, the Golds had repeatedly approached the owner with offers to purchase his property for sums which gradually escalated to completely unrealistic amounts. Ben was unfamiliar with the property, which was clearly unusual, but estimated its market value at the time in question to have been roughly one third of what the Golds were prepared to pay. Their efforts eventually ceased, presumably on receipt of a curt letter from the owner threatening legal action for harassment. This letter sat on top of the pile and, Anna saw, bore Nils' distinctive signature. She turned the correspondence over, glancing through it, but it offered no explanation as to why the Golds had been trying so hard to buy the cave house. And why hadn't Nils agreed to sell for such a huge sum of money? As none of this was Anna's business she felt she couldn't ask him about it, but the questions nagged at the back of her mind.

On her return from town, she saw he had washed bed linen, using the antiquated machine in an outhouse on the terrace, and spread it to dry over chairs and the wooden table. He was busy writing again and affected not to hear her approach. She made them coffee and a sandwich each then went for a shower. She was glad of the evening's planned meeting with her friends and the chance to catch up with other people's gossip.

Nils had been unable to voice any objection to her evening at Los Dos Caracoles as he planned to dine over a business meeting in Mange Tak which had also been scheduled for tonight. He was to pick her up in Palma Nova around midnight.

***

'Hello you! I've saved you a seat.' Maggie took her bag off the chair between herself and Jane and Anna sat down.

It was over a week since she'd spoken to Maggie and a lot had happened since then. Glancing at a menu, even though she knew the restaurant's fare off by heart, she agreed to the usual shared paella, a carafe of red, a carafe of white and bottles of agua sin gas.

There were normally six friends round the table, sometimes seven or eight. Tonight, besides Maggie and Jane, there was Sandra, who lived with her parents and taught English while bringing up her young son. Next to her was Liz, whose husband Pepe was the owner of a local nightclub generally considered to owe its success to Liz's hostessing skills. Then there was Sam, who lived in a modern but cramped apartment with Spanish waiter Miguel and their baby, Benny.

Maureen and her daughter Jill were not here tonight. They lived a frugal lifestyle owing to Maureen having been confused by the number of noughts on the deeds when selling a property in Spanish pesetas twenty years ago. This catastrophe had resulted in furious and unsympathetic family members back in England ceasing to visit and virtually disowning their impoverished relative.

'Jane's told me about the garage,' Maggie said. 'Is everything all right? You didn't ring.'

'Sorry Maggie but everything's happened so fast. It's all worked out okay though.'

Los Dos Caracoles was packed. Pavement stalls gradually multiplying in the vicinity were attracting more and more holidaymakers, all eager to purchase beach towels, giant inflatables, cheap souvenirs and printed t-shirts.

Inside the restaurant, smells of after sun preparations and duty free perfume mingled with the smoky smells of charred meat and grilled fish. Conversation was held in a mixture of languages interrupted by spontaneous bursts of laughter and the sudden flashes of numerous photographs being taken. These frequently featured raised glasses, reddened faces, peeling shoulders and grinning waiters.

'Isn't it noisy in here tonight?' Anna raised her voice above the restaurant's din.

'Come on, we're all waiting to hear about the mystery man. Are you living with him?' Sandra wanted to know.

'Only temporarily, while the power's off in my block.'

'What does he do?' Liz was curious.

'He was a farmer in Denmark and now he owns a restaurant here and researches articles about food and things for a Scandinavian institute. He likes opera and cooking. He's got a cat and a little dog.'

'Very self-sufficient; what does he need a woman for?' Jane asked, teasingly.

'Shut up,' said Anna good-humouredly.

The waiter arrived to take orders.

'What's the great Dane doing tonight? Is he working in the restaurant?' Liz wanted to know.

'He's there for some sort of business meeting . . . and

he's writing an article at the moment on depleted fish stocks in the North Sea.'

'Word has it, fish are still there; they're just lying low under the oil rigs and hiding out round the wind farms,' Jane quipped.

Anna had to laugh. 'That joke's been done to death . . . and what did you think of him?'

'Bit old, not bad looking, in fact I've found a picture of him.' Jane drew a folded cutting from *Meridian* out of her pocket. 'It was in that box of back numbers you gave me, from about three and a half years ago. Golds must have still been accessing the garage for storage.'

'It's possible,' said Anna. 'My parents never mentioned anything about having a garage so I didn't take any notice of it.'

Maggie leant over and she and Anna read the short piece which was accompanied by a headshot of Nils and a separate grainy picture of a woman.

Local Danish Restaurant Owner Reports Wife Missing.

'Nils Christiansen, a local restaurateur, has reported his wife, Eva, to local police as a missing person.

As well as owning Scandinavian restaurant Mange Tak in San Augustin, Mr Christiansen is also an authority and respected author of various papers on North Sea species, including: 'The North Sea; a Chemical Cocktail' and 'One hundred and Seventy Species of Fish and Other Life Forms'.

Mrs Christiansen, an acclaimed local artist,

lives with her husband in the Terreno district of Palma and also has a studio in the city. She was last seen in San Augustin on the morning of December 13th. Would anyone with any information regarding her whereabouts please contact the police station in Palma or get in touch with a member of staff at Meridian at the earliest possible opportunity.

Eva Christiansen is Danish and has long blonde hair. Unfortunately only a rather blurred photograph of her was available at the time of going to press.

Her husband, who reported her missing, has told police he is unable to assist with their enquiries in any way and simply wants to establish that his wife is safe and well.'

'Did she turn up?' Maggie asked the obvious question, looking from Jane to Anna.

'I've no idea. He's never mentioned her. Can we ask the magazine?' Anna squinted at the blurred photograph, trying to imagine the absent Eva.

'I doubt it. This by-line names someone I've never heard of and it's over three and a half years old.' said Jane. 'I did a quick search for a follow-up and couldn't find anything. Can't you ask Nils?'

'I could try. He's very private over personal things and I've only known him for a few weeks.' Anna hesitated. 'I might if the mood's right or I suppose I could ask his business partner if I could get him on his own. He must have known Eva.'

'Well someone must know what happened to her.

Keep the article and report back. If I can find anything out I'll let you know.' Jane grinned. 'Perhaps she's in the bat-cave with Robin.'

'Stop calling it that, you'll give me nightmares,' said Anna uneasily.

The meal was served and everyone filled their plates. Anna didn't finish her food and drank rather more wine than usual. What had become of Eva? And why had Nils turned down the Golds' astonishing offer for the cave house? She found his old-fashioned courtesy and formality rather endearing but in return it created a slight barrier of deference to him. Shades of Mr Lovatt the headmaster again; it would never be easy to question him on aspects of his life which were really no one else's business.

Before the evening was over, Anna was further disturbed by some revelations from Zhu, who had asked Jane to pass them on. Taking a private moment, Jane lowered her voice. 'By the way, Zhu knew Eva, she was a regular client at the salon until one day she missed an appointment and never came back. I'm sorry Anna, but Zhu remembers her being worried about her husband.'

'What did she mean, "worried about"?'

'Well, they were estranged and Eva thought he was following her. Zhu remembers her quite well. Eva was an artist and she gave Zhu a couple of signed paintings. One's in the apartment, you probably haven't noticed it, there's so much stuff on the walls. It's in the living area behind where Nils was sitting the other night; some sort of dragon, Zhu likes things like that.'

Anna didn't know what to say. Jane carried on.

'Zhu was very unsettled that night you came, she was going on about Nils' aura; she could hear someone crying. She's good at that stuff . . . honestly. I know this sounds weird but she says Nils has an old dark soul. She said there's an otherness somewhere that she can't quite put a name to. A bit creepy, eh?'

At this point Anna was relieved to be interrupted by the waiter clearing the table. She would never say anything to offend Jane or discredit Zhu's intuition but her brain felt overloaded by all today's unexpected information.

She said 'I haven't time for another coffee because Nils is picking me up, but thanks for looking out for me. Tell Zhu I do value her insight on things and I won't forget what she's said. I'll talk to you both very soon.'

'Take care, speak soon,' said Jane.

Maggie placed a hand on Anna's arm and kissed her cheek.

Nils' car was parked in the road outside. His meeting had gone well and his mood was upbeat. Might this be a good time to ask him about his missing wife, without referring to the old magazine article? Then, as he drove, Nils himself provided a conversational opening.

'You should have accompanied me tonight; I would like us to be seen as a couple. We are a couple, are we not? We should do everything together, no?' He squeezed Anna's hand.

'Yes, I'd like that.' Then she heard herself saying, 'You are divorced, aren't you?'

'I am becoming divorced. So we are free.' Nils' eyes were on the winding coast road as gaudily lit bars and restaurants streamed past. Snatches of popular music carried through the open car windows.

'Where does your ex-wife live?'

'I know where she is and you have no need to know. She is gone, so we will not speak of her.'

For now, it seemed that particular freight of exposition had pulled into a station. Anna was left to deduce that the mysterious Eva was no longer missing and further questions would have to wait.

About an hour later she went to bed, dimly aware of Nils' operatic music rising then falling into a soft lament. She was nearly asleep when Nils came in and sat for a moment on the edge of the bed. Fat church candles guttered on either side of the huge mirror and through half-open lids Anna's eyes fell on the reflection. Rainbows like diesel oil in puddles wavered round the edges. The blemished surface cast the illusion of scales or liver-spots across the skin on Nils' back. It was like looking through a dirty, rain spattered window-pane; Anna turned away. Nils rose to extinguish the candles and the room and its contents were enveloped in soft warmth and darkness.

***

Sleep quickly claimed Anna. She found herself back in her apartment in Palma Nova. The lights were out and it was in complete darkness. Of course, she rationalised, the electricity's off, the whole block's empty; perhaps that's why it's unusually cold, almost frosty in fact.

Then she heard a low scraping noise. Her imagination saw strong claw-like nails being drawn

slowly across a rough hard surface. It repeated again and again, building, until the air was filled with an unbearable screeching. Anna clenched her teeth as she desperately forced a finger in each ear. Stumbling in the darkness, heading for the faint blur of green-hued moonlight through glass, she made her way to the balcony door. She wrenched it open using one hand, trying to shield her unprotected ear against her shoulder.

Outside, an unfamiliar, ghostly moon-shadow was cast across the ground below and when Anna looked sideways she saw the Dragon clinging to the outside of the building. He was dragging his claws slowly and purposefully down the wall, creating tiny sparks which flew from the scored concrete like fireflies in the dark.

Anna knew instinctively he was aware of her but he was not distracted, only extending the reach of his claws further and further. The high-pitched noise was intolerable and Anna's eyes were screwed tightly shut, but her last sense before waking was that, mingled strangely with the smell of the sea, was the strong scent of apples.

***

She woke damp with perspiration in a tangled sheet, to find Nils, unusually for him, snoring on the other side of the bed. She carefully untangled herself and went to the fridge for a bottle of water. She peered out onto the terrace, but a stream of silver moonlight was quiet and serene; nothing stirred.

CHAPTER 10
HERE BE DRAGONS

August slipped by, uneventful and heavy with heat. Anna was satisfied with the progress of her book and also happy with her life with Nils. She occasionally stole into the luxurious hotel below, slipping past its wealthy patrons to access the hotel pool, always knowing the day she was approached and asked for her room number would be the day of her final swim. She was aware Nils didn't approve of this practice but pretended not to notice; a pool was one thing he was unable to offer his guest.

She had gradually become aware that although always appearing in public in a freshly laundered shirt, short sleeved in summer, long in winter, in private he much preferred the ease and practicality of nudity. She had caught him on a number of occasions padding about the terrace wearing only a tattered straw hat and worn leather sandals, and was aware it was out of deference to her that he mostly wore a thin cotton nightshirt or a pair of khaki shorts. Their outdoor lifestyle was overlooked only by the blind eyes of unglazed windows on the abandoned terraces above; witnessed only by seabirds riding high over the bay like motes of cloud suspended in the rays of the sun.

Visits to restaurants and bars, and to the nearest supermarket, were more about the new intimacy of coupledom than an exercise in what to wear and who might notice. Anna no longer took work to do in the Internet Café, only sharing a sofa there with Nils when the two of them went into town to shop together.

Jane escaped the city heat by flying to England to visit her parents, or mater and pater as she liked to call them; no affectation, just a joke.

Anna was planning to invite Maggie out for lunch when her mobile went. Maggie had called her.

'Anna I've something important to tell you. Can we get together or shall I tell you over the phone?'

'Let's do both. I was going to suggest a get-together anyway. I'm sitting here with writer's block, so . . . what's important?'

'Well, last week Javier's estate agency learnt an empty building in Palma Nova was under investigation for aluminosis. I was worried and checked…I'm afraid it's your block, Anna. Did you know? Had anyone told you?'

No one had, but everyone on the island knew all about aluminosis. It was rarely identified but the spectre of a possible indictment citing aluminosis hung over all the old builds in the area. It applied when a corrosive reaction occurred between aluminium and concrete, rendering the structure potentially unsafe. If reported to the local authority, the building could be condemned unless costly refurbishment was under-taken. There was no defence against the condition, no affordable insurance and only meagre financial compensation.

Spanish families accepted the situation as a consequence of living in relatively cheap accommodation.

Aluminosis was simply mal suerte, bad luck, an act of God.

'Oh no, what should I do?' Anna was horrified.

'I'm on my way into town. Are you on your own? I can meet you in the Internet Café in about an hour's time if you like,' Maggie said.

'Thanks Maggie. Nils has gone to an out of town market somewhere with Holger. He won't be back until this afternoon. See you in an hour.'

Anna hurried to leave. Would Maggie have any advice? Why hadn't she been notified by Señor Martínez? What would she do if the building was condemned? Actually, she knew the answer was fairly obvious, but didn't want to confront it just yet.

The café was filled with unfamiliar faces in August. Spanish businesses closed and those who were able to do so vacated the city, leaving it to the tourists, the extranjeros; the foreigners. Glad to be somewhere with air conditioning, Anna was impatient for Maggie's advice.

'I made a few enquiries before I left,' Maggie said, 'apparently the electricians found aluminosis and reported it. It was confirmed two days ago so there might be something in the post. Did you leave a forwarding address?'

'No!' Anna wailed. 'It's been confirmed. What happens now? At the moment I don't have enough money to buy another apartment. If this book does well, I might, but it's a very big 'if'.

'Well first of all, see what your administrator has to say,' said Maggie. 'It partly depends on what the other residents want to do; if no one wants to spend on refurbishing, well . . . you can always rent somewhere else. I could help you find somewhere cheap. There'll be some sort of compensation, although my guess is you'll have to wait ages. But couldn't you just stay on with Nils? Cut your losses; move in properly? You like being there, don't you? How's it going with you two?'

'Very well as it happens . . . but I didn't foresee this.'

'Of course you didn't, but things will work out. You wouldn't want to go back to England, would you? Drink that latte and relax. Go to see your administrator, what's his name, Martinez? Javier knows him. Oh, and Javier said if there's any compensation going, make sure you get more for the garage.'

'Thanks Maggie. Nils has been wanting me to move in properly, perhaps he'll get what he wished for.' Anna sipped her latte.

Maggie had another suggestion. 'There's a really popular fortune teller doing the circuit round the English hotels. I'd love a session. Shall we go together? You're supposed to book in advance. What do you think, shall I book?'

'Oh, all right. I've had the bad news, perhaps I'll get some good news.'

'Great. I'll check the dates and get back to you. Now I'm sorry but I'll have to go, loads to do . . . I can drop you in Terreno.'

'Thanks but now I'm here, I'll do some errands then I'll ask Nils to take me to Palma Nova later; find out what's going on. At least I'm lucky with my friends.' Anna managed a weak smile.

'I'd take you if I hadn't arranged to collect the boys and some of their friends. I've promised McDonalds then crazy golf. But anyway, I think involving Nils is a good idea, so he appreciates the problem.' Maggie was always pragmatic.

It was the start of the siesta by the time Anna returned to Terreno. Shops were shut and the old buildings baked silently in the dry heat as she entered the alleyway. The air was filled with cooking smells and her feet disturbed the scattered rubbish which whispered and crackled underfoot, occasionally stabbing her bare toes. She picked a thorny branch of bougainvillea from overhead and sucked her thumb where it had drawn blood. This was not a good day.

Back on the terrace, she dropped on to the blue beach towel covering the old settee and kicked off her sandals. She plucked her damp t-shirt and shorts away from her body, ran her fingers through her hair and shaded her eyes. Filmy white trails of exhaust criss-crossed the sky. They marked routes to destinations in which she had no interest; she was where she wanted to be. She could even contemplate staying here forever if that was what fate decreed.

The view dazzled like a silvered mirror-image, a fractured reflection of light and movement. From the far right and the rotund battlements of the fourteenth-century Castell de Bellver, the eye was drawn downwards around the whole curve of the Bay of Palma, then back again along the horizon, past the silhouettes of giant tankers ferrying precious cargoes of fresh water to the island.

To the left sat the gothic cathedral, Sa Seu; a sandstone edifice Nils stubbornly refused to admire, citing the vast numbers of black slaves who had perished labouring on its construction.

'Denmark was the very first country to abolish slavery,' was one of his proud boasts. History was one of his favourite subjects and Anna had often noticed, despite having a number of Spanish friends, he could be quite judgemental of his adopted countrymen.

Actually he could be quite judgemental of most people. He sometimes quoted one of Denmark's old Jante laws, 'Don't think you are better than anybody else': this he claimed was strictly adhered to by Danish citizens, although of course, he added, it obviously related to fellow Danes and not to other races such as the Spanish.

Anna was often unsure whether Nils was serious or amusing himself by teasing her, but she was confident he was serious about their relationship and he did encourage her writing, even though his own was very different. She liked the way he loved the real heart of the island, its old and secret places where nature still ruled and the way he enjoyed sharing them with her. True, he was older than her . . . but so what?

She sometimes speculated what her parents would have thought of him. She knew that as her daughter progressed through her thirties without a long-lasting committed relationship, her mother had resigned herself to a life without grandchildren; although she herself had had Anna relatively late in life. She had accepted the situation long before her life was extinguished by her weak heart. But Anna couldn't help thinking that Nils' old-fashioned courtesy would have won her mother over in spite of his age.

Her father would have kept his views to himself,

trusting that time would tell, making no secret of the fact that women in general and his daughter in particular were something of an enigma.

Nils did warrant the approval of Señor Martínez when he drove Anna to Palma Nova later that day. In the car he had maintained a sympathetic silence, occasionally taking his hand off the steering wheel to pat her knee, kept company by his own thoughts.

First they visited Anna's apartment block, now a rather sorry sight. It was still festooned with black cables, now more exposed and complemented by generous lengths of black and yellow sticky tape, indicating a hazard. A prominently displayed notice warned 'PELIGRO/DANGER'. There was no sign of life apart from a thin tortoiseshell cat sitting washing its dusty fur. It occurred to Anna that the building looked rather like an intensive care patient, hooked up to hidden equipment and swathed in coloured bandages. She didn't get out of the car.

Señor Martínez didn't keep them waiting before delivering a prognosis. Having first ushered them through to his office with ceremonious hand-sweeping gestures, he then offered plastic cups of water from a cooler behind the door. Anna hadn't noticed this before and had certainly never been offered any water from it.

Never having shown much respect for the unmarried English woman, Señor Martínez was clearly impressed with her Danish partner who spoke good Spanish. He addressed most of the conversation to him. Anna had long ago reluctantly resigned herself to Latino machismo, having discovered the best result was obtained by not fighting it. She listened without interruption.

The Spanish residents had accepted the situation which was, make no mistake, muy mal, very bad, and dispersed themselves amongst various grandparents, brothers, sisters and cousins. They regarded any compensation, however slight, as good fortune and perhaps the señora should cultivate this positive attitude. Did the señora's insurance cover aluminosis? No . . . well then . . . And what if a workman had been injured or worse, who would have helped his family? The notario crossed himself at the thought. One should think of such things.

The apartment must be cleared of possessions immediately, before any more risks were taken and then further assessment could begin. Community meetings would cease until further notice.

Aware of her altered status from señorita to señora, Anna listened as Nils assured the notario she had somewhere to live but would need to be kept informed of the situation, giving his address and phone number. She was able to offer no alternative solution other than the unattractive prospect of searching quickly for an apartment for rent and experienced an attack of inertia at the mere thought of it. As the shock of the bad news subsided and the simple solution was established, relief percolated through her system. After all, she could still move whenever she wanted to, couldn't she?

Eventually Señor Martínez bowed them out of his office with further obsequious gestures and hand-shakes. He would be in touch when matters were settled.

As shops re-opened after the siesta, readying themselves for the anticipated evening tourist trade, Nils and Anna walked for a while then sat down at a pavement café overlooking the promenade. There was always a lull while holidaymakers deserted the beach for hotel dining rooms, ready to eat before taking a leisurely stroll in the balmy evening air.

Nils commented on the intricate mosaic of the pavements where brick and cream coloured floral designs swirled at his feet like giant poinsettias. They were, he noted, very like the pavements in Palma's most prestigious shopping precinct, the Galerias. Anna smiled.

'The famous Palma Nova pavements. The council laid new road surfaces here a few years ago but rather than take up the old surface first, the workmen laid new tarmac on top of it. The roads ended up higher than the pavements so when it rained, the run-off flowed into the shops. By then the council were paving in Palma, they sent some paving from there back here to raise the pavement levels above the road again.'

Nils looked from the highly decorative paving to Anna. 'Is that so? You are very well informed.'

'Not really. I've lived here a while now . . . but I seem to be moving on.'

'Indeed. We must arrange for your household belongings to be collected and delivered to my home.'

'Where will we store them?'

'Do not concern yourself. I have plenty of storage space; along the terrace, behind the bath-room, you will be surprised.'

'Actually most of the furniture was my parents, it's quite old and I'm not really bothered about keeping it. Although, I suppose, it still needs disposing of.' A sudden wash of nostalgia stung the backs of Anna's eyes.

'We have at our disposal the van from Mange Tak.'

‘Will it be large enough though?’ said Anna dubiously, adding, ‘I know someone with a furniture van.’

‘Who is this?’

‘His name’s Jamil. He owns an antique shop in the Galerias.’

‘Ah, I believe I may have seen you there. But his items are most expensive . . . you are a customer?’

‘Not exactly, I first visited the shop on behalf of a friend. Actually Jamil’s paid me to help him out on a couple of occasions; liaising with clients.’

‘Like a secretary or a personal assistant, perhaps?’

‘Sort of . . . I’ve already agreed to help him one day next week. I hope that’s alright. He’s going somewhere to collect some carpets and it’s a castle and I’m getting on really well with my book but I’d love to visit a castle I can describe. I won’t need any more characters or inspirations after that. Say it’s not a problem. I can arrange for him to have the apartment cleared and dispose of what I don’t want, which would be really useful.’

‘This will be your last time with this man?’

‘If that’s what you want. If you continue to absolutely refuse rent, I can live on less money.’

‘We shall manage very well and you do not need to iron for the one they call Red.’

‘No, I suppose I don’t.’

‘Well then, once again we agree. I am very happy and we must celebrate. Your birthday is soon, is it not?’

‘Don’t remind me.’

‘Ah-ha, a big one, yes?’

Anna grimaced. The only slight consolation in being

forty in two weeks' time would be that no matter what her age, she would always be considerably younger than Nils.

***

That night, after Anna went to bed with a book, the bedroom candles quivered beside the speckled Florentine mirror. It reflected Nils' discarded leather sandals. The worn and frayed piece of Persian carpet on which they lay turned to baked terracotta pavements whose spiralling mosaics were blood-red starfish; they reached blindly out towards a sea where the waves crashed and boiled, rising upwards. The air became dark and churned wildly as great gales came banging in from all around.

Anna's book fell to the floor with a thump and she awoke, startled. Nils was approaching the bed where she had fallen asleep and begun to dream. He climbed in beside her.

'You were dreaming?'

'Yes, the sea was thrashing about and rising up like some sort of monster. It was unreal.'

'Oh no, it is real; at Skagen, at the northernmost tip of Denmark, at the junction of the northern seas. The Baltic waters of the Kattegat collide most violently with the spring tides of the Skagerrak. The waters seethe and fight, up to twenty-five metres high, and great sandstorms sweep across the peninsula.'

'Goodness, how frightening. Have you been there?'

'I have been many times. The air is charged, its essence enters your psyche. The old maps say there are dragons there.'

'Dragons!' Anna gathered the bedcover around herself.

'Indeed. Jormungand, the Midgard Serpent writhes as she makes her way towards land. It is said the waves will set free the ship Naglfar, a ship of giants, and a second ship also will set sail from the realms of the dead.'

'Is it always so wild . . . where the dragons are?'

'No, not quite; there are six days each year of dead calm.'

'Perhaps the dragons need to sleep.' Anna thought of Trog and his unmade bed. 'Perhaps the sea flat-lines for them.'

***

The Dragon listened and considered this concept with interest, his eyes sly and sharp. Certainly the sea accommodated his needs and housed others like himself, although he had never met the Midgard Serpent and had no particular wish to do so.

He himself possessed the ability to absorb energy when naturally occurring elements on Earth caused powerful temporal fissures in time and space and he could slip unnoticed through the crack, past human vision, recharging and conserving his power.

He also knew of other dragons recorded by the ancients. One such Norse dragon was Nidhogg, who lived beneath Yggdrasil, the guardian tree at the axis of the world. He was known as the corpse-sucker on Nastrond, the shore of corpses.

The Dragon preferred his own gelid habitats to those of the charnel house and had never met Nidhogg either. Their realms were apart and separate; although the Dragon did not doubt Nidhogg's existence; but humans were so much more

entertaining alive than dead.

He had indeed first encountered Nils in Skagen's maelstrom. The man had stood his ground, damming the gods on that wild spit of land, surrounded by gulls screeching into the wind, his aura flawed and fascinating. The Dragon knew Nils' was one of many pale shades still drifting there, restive and unquiet.

CHAPTER 11
A CASTLE

'Vaya con Dios!'

As Anna entered the antique shop, the old-fashioned door-bell jangled on its coiled spring and Lorca, the African grey parrot, conferred his usual benediction to go with God, oblivious as to whether those passing his cage were coming or going.

'Good morning Lorca. Is Jamil here?'

Jamil stepped out from beside one of his carpets, which was draped over a high-backed chair covered in black and white cowhide. This was positioned behind a heavy looking table studded with large-headed hobnails. As Jamil walked forward, a young dark-skinned assistant silently materialised to stand in his place. The manoeuvre was executed like a stage-managed illusion.

'Good morning, Anna. On time and looking beautiful as usual. Please . . . follow me.'

Anna blinked in the dim light and breathed in an aroma of exotic incense. 'Good morning; I'm not late, am I?'

'No, but you would have been worth waiting for.' He raised Anna's hand and pressed it to his lips, then in a business-like fashion ushered her back outside and across the pavement to where a large powerful car was parked on double yellow lines.

As the shop interior fell silent again, Lorca ruffled his feathers, scratched his head and closely inspected the piece of breakfast banana Jamil had pushed into his cage.

Jamil's young male assistant retreated into a backroom, the dusty corners of which were stacked with alabaster angels, swaged stone urns and ornamental figurines. Here lay the baby Jesus, cradled in the arms of his mother, and there, a representation of a crucifix encrusted with coloured stones caught in a shaft of light. A few chalices and goblets sat tumbled in a wooden box and, on the walls, sad-looking saints bestowed their blessings from canvases and wooden panels. On unlit racks of shelving, assorted dusty reliquaries secretively guarded their contents and, in one corner, a hushed trio of skulls grinned in unison.

In the centre of the room, beneath naked light bulbs which hung on long flexes decorated by the work of numerous spiders, a large table served as Jamil's desk; an island of order and technology, arranged with leather-bound books, ledgers, a computer screen, keyboard and printer and a closed laptop.

Peeling wooden window shutters were unfolded and secured across the windows, beneath which, flaking window ledges were places where cigarettes were stubbed out and trapped insects perished seeking the light.

All a little too crypt-like, Anna had told herself, on the only occasion on which she had ventured inquisitively into this room. She would have loved to explore but was quickly informed that the office and stock-room were out of bounds unless by appointment. Slightly put out by this rebuff, she had ignored the room's existence ever since.

Anna had travelled in Jamil's car before but it never failed to impress her with its luxurious interior. As the doors locked, a gentle cooling airflow washed over its passengers like balm, a welcome contrast to the heat of August. It purred its way through the early traffic and as Anna settled back into her seat she was treated to the feel and smell of expensive leather upholstery the colour of melted butter.

She glanced sideways at Jamil's elegant manicured hands on the steering wheel. His wrists disappeared into crisp white shirt cuffs which he had adjusted meticulously before starting the car. He wore monogrammed cufflinks but Anna couldn't decipher the initials; she'd never known Jamil's surname. It crossed her mind that these were the sort of details Nils would frown at and therefore, ones he would never hear from her.

She'd avoided telling him the exact role she played in helping Jamil, who today had plans to visit a potentially important client on the other side of the island. He wanted Anna to accompany him, posing as his English business partner, and for this service he always paid a generous commission.

She believed she understood Jamil. Insecure and self-conscious, an adult son still living under the roof of his wealthy parents, he was uncomfortable visiting clients in their own homes, particularly if the client was a woman. In spite of his appreciation of fine art, business acumen and expertise in his field, something in his appearance or nervous demeanour made people mistrustful of him. Worse still, as soon as he perceived this reaction, he was inclined to start behaving defensively, so appearing even more untrustworthy.

Anna knew he valued her image of Britishness and simple friendliness, seeing in it the perfect foil for the foreignness he perceived within himself. Her knowledge of the goods in which he dealt was sketchy but he knew she was genuinely interested, and that she could make herself available at short notice, while her appreciating a little financial help had made the arrangement perfect.

Anna was considering how to find a way of telling him this would be their last trip together. She hoped they would find something to talk about as chanting voices and tinkling music from the stereo conjured a picture of wind chimes in a sunny English garden and were exerting a hypnotic influence. To fall asleep would be embarrassing.

Jamil spoke. 'I'm told you've moved house, Anna. I believe your friend is Danish but I see you haven't yet made a commitment.' His gaze shifted momentarily to Anna's hands, which rested in her lap. She immediately rearranged them, feeling betrayed by her ringless fingers.

'How did you know? Who told you?'

'I have many contacts in the city.' Jamil sounded amused. 'Would you like to meet some of the people I do business with, later today? You may find them interesting. They only speak Spanish of course but you should learn, Anna. You English are lazy with languages.'

'I know; I feel suitably chastised. It's on my to-do list.' Anna watched as the glitzy colours of top-end commerce gave way to the monochromes of the highway leading them out of the city.

Jamil answered his own question. 'You can come with me when we return, my friends are here in the city.

But meanwhile, are you still writing your book?'

'Yes I am. All my characters are established now and the story's coming together nicely. I'm doing some illustrations but the main characters need a castle and I'm struggling to get it just right.'

'Have you visited the Castell de Bellver? It is quite close to your new address.'

'Yes, but it's empty and hollow, as if no one ever lived there . . . like a fort. To be honest I'm hoping for some ideas today. I've brought a sketch-book. You did say we were visiting a castle?'

'We are indeed.' Jamil explained that today's client was a wealthy widow, an elderly member of the Spanish aristocracy who lived in a large castellated building furnished with valuable carpets and wall-hangings, a number of which she wished to sell. He believed that by presenting Anna as an associate or business partner he could win the client's confidence and strike a better deal. He fully expected to return to the city with a well stacked roof-rack or, at least, arrangements to revisit the widow in a larger van.

Anna remembered to mention her parent's furniture and Jamil promised some transport and two of his employees. They could drop off her selection of items at her new address and dispose of the remainder. Envisaging the impasse of Torreno's narrow alleyways encouraged Anna to plan to keep as little as possible.

'Actually I think I'll just lock anything I want to keep inside the garage first then your men can simply clear whatever remains. That keeps it simple; in fact here's a spare key.' She rummaged inside her purse and placed a key in a compartment on the dashboard. 'Give me until the end of the week then send them round. I'll pop in the shop sometime and pick up the key. And thank you so much.'

Jamil nodded his head in confirmation. He drove in a northerly direction, through the tiny hamlet of Establiments heading towards Esporles, passing through the dip in the island's mountainous backbone, the Serra de Tramuntana. As they approached the coast, where the serried terraces of Banyalbufar lay ahead to the left, they turned right in the direction of Valldemossa.

'The scenery up here's really beautiful,' said Anna, as both the car and the temperature outside it rose higher and higher. 'Is there much further to go?'

'I thought we might stop near Valldemossa for some late lunch, a Menu del Dia, then continue on a little further afterwards. Our client lives between there and Deiá. How does that sound?'

'Lovely. Does she really live in a castle? Is she very rich?'

'Don't you know, Anna; this island's past has created many wealthy women? Years ago, when peasant farmers scratched their livings here, they bequeathed what arable land they had to their sons. To their daughters they bequeathed areas of coastline, useless for cultivation. Then the tourists came. Suddenly the coastline was much sought-after by property developers and the farmer's daughters became rich overnight. They were able to marry into wealthy families and lived happily ever after.'

'Oh, what a good plot for a story; I wish I'd been a Mallorcan farmer's daughter.' Anna imagined how she might have lived on unexpected wealth as the car slowly pulled in to a small market square.

Jamil parked opposite a long low terraced restaurant with shaded tables out on the cobbled paving stones. Waiters observed the unfamiliar car and slipped into sight, hopeful of generous customers. They showed them to the best table, where they ate sobrasada, a paprika sausage, with rustic bread, crushed tomatoes and garlic. Jamil ordered a mixed platter of cucumber, tomatoes, dates, boiled eggs, goat's cheese and watermelon.

Anna secretly felt a little guilty and disloyal to be enjoying an outing so much without Nils.

After lunch, they left behind the cobbled streets and stone houses with their neat corrugated tile roofs, driving higher, past scattered daub and wattle outbuildings and small shelters, until eventually Jamil turned off the road.

Lower down, they had passed through pasture-land dotted with almond trees, olive and citrus groves and now everywhere were the pines which made the island so green. Bushy stone pines clung to rocky outcrops of land, maritime pines leaned at precarious angles and small fan-shaped palms spiked the contours of the dry uneven ground.

As the car slowly followed an unmarked track through low juniper and lavender and down a wooded slope, Anna realised this was the drive leading to their destination. Here and there a fine mesh was draped across bushes and strung between the lower branches of trees, resembling aerial tennis nets.

'What are all these nets for?'

'Birds, mainly thrushes.' Jamil glanced at her. 'For

food. The people here are poor Anna, they live off the land. You Anna are not poor, but you enjoy dishes made with duck or chicken. The English celebrate with pheasant and roast turkey, do they not? The Scottish have their grouse, I believe.'

'How do they work?'

'They are spread with glue.'

Anna gasped in horror. She stared at the nets, at what she had taken to be dark clumps of trapped leaves and felt her throat constrict. Unable to think of a satisfactory reply, she pressed her lips together and studied her freshly painted finger nails.

Sensing her discomfort, Jamil added, 'These so-called parany traps are illegal and if caught, the hunters can face considerable fines and a criminal record. They take the risk to feed their families.'

A few moments later, the castle Anna had come for revealed itself. It was perfect. A large grey box shaped construction like a French chateau or small monastery with a castellated roof and here and there, small turrets.

Jamil parked on the track and took his silver-grey suit jacket and a slim-line briefcase from the back seat. He had explained to Anna that some elderly Spanish people could feel intimidated by, or suspicious of, a display of technology such as a laptop. He adjusted his shirt cuffs with a self-conscious tugging motion.

Anna hastily applied more lip gloss and checked her hair in the illuminated mirror behind the sun visor. She smoothed the skirt of her cream linen suit and stepped out of the car, reaching back in to gather her jacket and her satchel containing sketch pad and pencils. She followed

Jamil across the gravel-strewn parking area and through an archway in an outer wall into a sunny courtyard.

On the crazed plaster of the surrounding walls were the faded remains of trompe l'oeil paintings depicting windows and doorways opening onto stylized formal gardens. At the centre of the courtyard was an old well shaft with a broken wooden lid. Groundcover of some sort of cacti spread out, reaching across the baked earth towards them. The vivid orange of its flowers climbed the walls beside grapevines which wound around the window grilles of small square windows with deep sills. On each side of a heavy oak door, surrounded by pots of pelargoniums, sat a stone cherub; one with no face and the other missing an arm and some toes.

The visitors must have been observed because as they approached, the door was opened slowly by the lady of the house herself; her thin body wrapped in a fringed black shawl with a mantilla loosely draped over severely scraped back hair. Anna thought she looked like an ancient flamenco dancer.

After an elaborate apology for it being the day the housekeeper visited her family in Son Moragues, introductions were made and Anna and Jamil were led into a huge reception area at least two storeys high. At the far end was a great open fireplace, near which high-backed tapestry-covered settles were arranged.

Following some polite small talk, the Spanish Condesa, expressing interest in Anna's side-line as a writer and aspiring illustrator, graciously gave permission for the Señora to sketch whilst she and Jamil went into an ante-room where the carpets for sale had been laid out.

Anna eagerly opened her sketch pad and began to draw. She sketched her impression of the picturesque courtyard with its old well. Then she drew the giant fireplace with its impossibly outsize set of fire-irons, thinking their dimensions would suit her Ogre. She drew her immediate surroundings, which were adorned on one side by uncomfortable-looking wrought iron chairs, inexplicably fixed in a horizontal row halfway up one wall, as if the floor beneath them had dropped away; perhaps it had; like something out of Alice in Wonderland, thought Anna.

Hanging by chains from low beams at different levels were Moroccan style lantern lights. Medieval looking branched candlesticks stood in corners on the flag-stoned floor beside terracotta urns filled with palms and cacti.

In the centre of the floor area a huge red-coloured carpet lay, protected by an opaque sheet of polythene which crackled when stood upon. Woven rugs and tapestries dressed the wall space. An intricately carved balcony or pulpit jutted out of one corner overhead and as Anna put the finishing touches to her drawing of its ornate mouldings she pictured the Wicked Queen poised there, plotting.

Jamil and their hostess re-appeared in the hall and Anna hastily rose to follow them, gingerly balanced on tiptoe, across the crackling polythene to sit on one of the uncomfortable tapestry covered settles.

A deal had evidently been done and at least one member of staff was working as tea was now served by an elderly man wearing what looked like a well-worn uniform belonging to someone a little larger. The translucent china teacups and saucers he set before the guests were marked with a gold crest.

Fifteen minutes later the same ageing retainer was summoned to help load Jamil's car. A young boy came with him and together they carried out an assortment of rolled and folded rugs and carpets, all destined to be reincarnated in Jamil's backstreet workshops.

Everyone seemed happy. The Condesa graciously requested a signed copy of Anna's completed book and waved regally from her doorstep as her visitors disappeared beyond the walled archway.

Jamil reversed the car and as they passed under trees Anna looked through the reflection of her face in the glass of the window. The nets had been relieved of their prey and she tried not to think of the fate of tomorrow's dawn chorus.

'I can hear the birds singing now,' she said, scanning the bushes.

'What you hear is a tape recording, a lure.' Jamil paused, then to distract her said: 'Now you will come to meet some of the other people I do business with. They source items from wealthy institutions and bring them to me for sale through my shop. You have indicated you no longer wish to accompany me on business trips, in order to comply with your new way of life, but who knows, you may change your mind and join me again in the future.'

'I suppose so. Are they around here . . . these people?'

'They are everywhere, but I told you Anna, they are in the city and they will make you welcome.'

CHAPTER 12
CLUES AND SECRETS

'Vaya con Dios!'

Lorca hung sideways from the bars of his cage, tipping his head up to squawk at the second visitor of the day.

Slightly taken aback by the unexpected greeting, Nils frowned at the bird then paused as a more thoughtful expression settled across his face. He surveyed his surroundings; the carpets, suspended like screens or draped across furniture like rich woven fabrics amid Moorish artefacts and vaguely religious icons. His nose wrinkled; the air was evocative of the scent of the souk.

'May I be of assistance?' The shop assistant wore a long loose garment, a djellaba, the traditional design and colours of the material blending him with his surroundings. He seemed to glide out of shadows as Nils' eyes adjusted from the searing brightness outside to the shop's low-lit interior.

Nils stepped forward. 'I do not wish to make a purchase today, only, perhaps, an enquiry.' He picked up a small olive wood box and paused to scrutinize its pearlised inlay, and then carefully returned the item to its position on a brass topped table.

'My employer is not here today; he has business on the other side of the island. However, I will assist in whatever way I am able.' The assistant spoke perfect English.

'Hmm,' said Nils. 'I encountered the proprietor of these premises whilst visiting a reclamation yard in search of building materials. If I am not mistaken, your employer was there negotiating a price for a statue, a representation of Jesus Christ offering benediction.'

The assistant inclined his head slightly without taking his eyes off his potential customer. He slid his hands into the sleeves of his garment and waited while Nils formulated his question.

'This would make a most attractive bird-bath, would it not?' Nils ran his fingers around the rim of a small stone font in which sat a potted aspidistra. 'I am at the moment furnishing a small chapel. It is on my property. It has a shrine and will be used for prayer and quiet contemplation, so I wish to create a suitable atmosphere. What can you show me? I would not argue with the price for the right kind of objects.'

The assistant continued to study his customer for a further few seconds, a shrewd expression in his dark brown eyes, then seeming to come to a decision he took a few steps back and motioned to Nils to follow him. He swept aside the curtain separating the shop from the back room. Then, standing to one side without speaking, he flicked the light switch and extended one arm out in an arc which encompassed all the room's contents. Motes of dust hung in the dry air, the room's items, disturbed unexpectedly, appeared transfixed in time. If Nils had not known Jamil was elsewhere, he might have expected to see him at his desk, having been seated there silently in the dark.

'Ah!' He adjusted his glasses and looked around keenly. His eyes picked out the dull gleam of tarnished silverware and the blank stares of the devout and the angelic. The skulls presided silently from their high shelf. 'Most interesting, yes, most interesting indeed.' After a few moments he stepped back into the shop. 'I have seen what I came for and now I will leave. Your stock has given me some ideas which I will take away with me and think about. Much of it originated in religious institutions, did it not?'

The assistant didn't answer.

'Such origins make it suitable for my chapel, of course.'

The assistant once more silently inclined his head whilst maintaining an inscrutable expression.

'Well, I will do any business transactions through the proprietor when he returns. I hope he is enjoying a most profitable day in the north of the island. Buenos dias.'

The assistant bowed slightly.

'Vaya con Dios!' squawked Lorca to Nils' retreating back.

The city streets looked washed and clean this early in the day. City people looked fresh and bright in their summer clothes. Some flicked and twittered, busy as brightly plumaged birds on pavements light-stippled through the overhead branches of plane trees. Others, with time to spare, watched the world pass by from in front of pavement cafés where the air smelled of percolating coffee and newly baked pastries. Delivery vans blocked side streets. Boxes were unloaded onto pavements, trays of patisserie carried aloft, sides of beef, lamb and pork wheeled on trolleys and lavish flower arrangements lifted with great care through narrow doorways.

Nils walked restlessly. He decided on a coffee and just as he did so, down one side street in the city's heart, there was Dali's, the favourite haunt of Jane and Zhu. He had not known where it was and now slowed his step to approach it cautiously. Inside, behind a café-curtain on a brass rod, apparently writing something in a notebook, sat Jane.

Nils automatically drew up in surprise, like a guilty party caught in the act, and at the same moment Jane looked up and saw him. There was a brief pause of recognition before she raised a coffee cup to beckon him inside to join her.

'Hello, what's the Great Dane up to today?' she said brightly, laying down her pen.

Nils hesitated beside the table, experiencing an internal struggle with the usual protocol. He arrived at a decision and bent to kiss Jane on both cheeks before seating himself opposite.

'Danish I am, certainly. Use of the word "great" is ambiguous.'

'It's a very big dog, actually.'

'So', Nils puzzled for a moment then gave up, adding, 'Anna is away on business and I too had business in town. I have never been in this restaurant.' He surveyed his surroundings. 'It is most unusual.'

Jane smiled. 'You mean the drawings?'

Nils ordered a café sin leche and another for Jane and stared around at the walls which were adorned on all sides with scraps and squares cut from paper table-covering, the rudimentary artwork of many customers.

'Is the service in this establishment very slow?'

Jane laughed out loud. Nils was puzzled again; he had not intended to joke.

'Why don't you try your hand?' Jane indicated the pot of pencils and crayons sitting in the centre of the table on its white paper cloth.

Nils inched away from them slightly, as if their proximity might cause a brightly coloured crayon to leap into his hand. 'Where is your, er . . . partner today?'

'Zhu? She works full-time at the salon in the hotel. I'll be popping in there later.'

Their coffees arrived and Jane closed her notebook, placing it on top of a small pile of similar notebooks next to her on the table. Nils watched her movements. On the night they met, the lights in the city apartment had been dimmed but now he observed that her creamy fair skin was scattered with freckles which accentuated her boyish look. In contrast to this he could also see, in her open-necked blue shirt, the cleavage between generous breasts which he had previously failed to notice. To Nils' eyes, nothing about her betrayed her sexual inclinations. She was attractive, brisk and cheerful. He experienced a warming sensation and shifted uncomfortably in his seat.

'I have, this morning, visited the shop of an acquaintance of Anna's. You may know it. The stock is of woven carpets and decorative items which I have reason to believe may be obtained dishonestly and therefore sold illegally.'

'Whoa there, steady on,' said Jane, 'don't forget you're talking to a reporter and Anna is a friend.'

'Ah, so,' Nils nodded. 'You are correct. We will talk of other subjects. What is your writing about?'

'I'm actually re-working some copy to fit onto a page. Are you writing any papers or anything at the moment? You were a farmer in Denmark, weren't you?'

'That is so. My field of interest naturally covers agricultural methods, but these have changed greatly. I study more the changing and collapsing ecology of the North Sea. It is both a tragic and fascinating subject. Do you know of the Norwegian Trench?'

'Sounds like a fish?'

Nils frowned. 'It is the deepest underwater channel known on the planet; a place where oils and minerals settle and ooze down into the so-called black zone where no life forms of any description can survive.'

'Lovely,' said Jane with a grimace.

'Also I have a great love of the Danish countryside, the flora and fauna, and of healthy nutrition. You must visit my restaurant, Mange Tak; you and your friend of course. I could introduce you to some Danish specialities.'

'Great,' said Jane. 'We'll arrange something; a foursome.'

Nils forced his gaze to avoid her blouse and concentrated on how the sunlight caught tiny golden hairs on her bare arms.

'Yes indeed. I have business in Copenhagen soon and will be absent for a few days but after I return . . . perhaps . . . may I ask you for your advice?'

'Of course, ask away.'

'It will be Anna's birthday soon and I wish to surprise her with a gift I have thought of. However I am unsure, as yet, of her taste in such things and wonder if you, her friend, would know better than I.'

'Go on,' Jane nodded.

'I have an idea to give her an amber necklace, of pieces of an irregular shape strung on silver. I think it would be correctly described as an artisan piece.'

'Amber, an ancient talisman, worn and traded across Europe by the Vikings,' said Jane, 'no two pieces alike; very apt and very beautiful. Lucky lady, I'm sure she'll absolutely love it.'

'Good, good.' Nils pictured smooth light pieces of warm amber dipping into the cleavage in front of him and hastily lifted his coffee cup.

'The news in Denmark is good,' said Jane.

Nils narrowed his eyes slightly while he studied Jane's face for clues as to which direction this conversation might take. Denmark's first woman prime minister, Helle Thorning-Schmidt, was celebrating the victory of a social coalition. They had overturned the centre-right and a decade of Liberal-Conservative rule. Was there an echo of the Red Stockings in the fact that she was known for wearing the colour red? Her nickname was Gucci Helle, with reference to her expensive tastes. The woman had a strident voice and a manner unbecoming in a female. Also it was common knowledge that her husband, the son of well-known British politicians from the eighties and three years her junior, was happy to operate as a house-husband, child-minding and cooking.

From Nils' perspective it was rather difficult to view all this as good news. Would someone like Jane, probably confused about their sexuality, be a feminist or be capable of more old-fashioned conservative views? What did the world look like through those lively hazel eyes? To know her better would have been interesting.

Nils pondered his own hypothetical questions for too long without offering Jane a response. She looked at him quizzically and moved on to a different subject.

'Your wife Eva used to come in here sometimes,' she said, taking Nils by surprise. 'I think I can find one of her drawings, she was quite good. Hang on a minute.'

'Hmm . . . yes.' Nils stiffened in his chair, eyes wandering to the walls around him. It was disquieting that traces of his ex-wife should, unbeknown to him, be on public display. Also, it was news to him that Anna's friends had known her. His hard-backed café chair was becoming uncomfortable.

Jane stood and crossed to a corner of the back wall where a folded lattice-work screen rested against the wall. For a few seconds she leafed through overlapping, fading pieces of paper, forgotten behind the screen, until one caught her eye.

'I thought so; this is hers,' she brought it back to the table and handed it to Nils. 'Have it if you want.'

Nils placed his reading glasses on the bridge of his nose and studied the picture. The scene was impressionistic. Dark green trees like heads of broccoli backed some sort of small red building. Stylised sun-rays beamed onto a field of tall waving flowers. Something about it increased his discomfort, although he wasn't sure what it was. It didn't look much like Eva's usual work, but he did recognise her hand and a scrawled signature across one corner was only too familiar.

'Keep it,' said Jane. 'They're public property really and they must be overdue for a good clear-out.'

Nils slowly folded his glasses; folded the drawing and placed it in the breast pocket of his blue checked shirt. He rose and extended a hand to Jane. Her grasp was firm and friendly, her smile open and engaging. He took the liberty of kissing her again on each cheek.

'We will meet again. I will look forward to it.'

'Say hello to Anna.'

'But of course.'

The morning seemed to have taken on a different atmosphere, and Nils' mood was reflective as he walked back the way he had come, past jewellers shops, clothing boutiques and delicatessens.

He drove to Terreno, turning things round in his mind. There was something else he wanted to do while Anna was out for the day.

***

The Dragon crouched on the terrace. He had planted the idea of the amber necklace, weevil-like, in Nils' mind. He liked amber. Its natural glowing warmth was the life-blood of the forests. Warm-blooded species owned only pathetic life-spans, while many trees survived for hundreds, even thousands of years with a chronology all their own, nourished by their secret amber sap. It contained the essence of the great Boreal forest belts which had encircled Earth's northern hemisphere with pines, firs and spruces when the Dragon was young. He had travelled through dark matter, bursting into the blinding white of rocks clothed in ice, softened by the living green.

The colour of amber represented strength and purpose in the human auras the Dragon saw. Its dominance in Nils' aura denoted the arrogance of an assumed charisma, an expectance of others doing things his way.

With Eva, the colour had denoted originality, evident in her artwork, and when mixed with green showed her to be relaxed and open to new opportunities. Later it had swirled with red, indicating a time of discovery, decisions and disorder.

Now Anna would have to learn about Eva before moving on to the Dragon's planned conclusion. He flared his nostrils and hissed at Tosca, who backed underneath a chair, spitting.

***

Nils prepared a lunch of smoked herring, green salad with radishes, and rye bread, which he ate thoughtfully, sitting on the terrace. Tosca sidled out of her hiding place, rejected a morsel of fish and settled down beside Nils' chair.

'Well Tosca, where is Puccini? I have not seen him for two days but his bowl is emptied, was that you or him? Now I have a job to do inside and you must stay outside in case we lose you, eh? We must make Anna happy; she will stay and when the time is right we will share our secret with her.'

He rose, entered through the French doors, closed them behind himself; crossed through the living space and bedroom and entered the bathroom. He reached up to a small ledge where the rock wall was rougher higher up, and took down a key, with which he unlocked the wooden door into the storage space behind the bathroom.

He located the battery-powered lantern suspended by wire from an overhang of rock and the cave was illuminated with a yellow wavering light. At the rear, a crevice or fissure in the rock receded backwards and remained in darkness, but the immediate area was revealed as storage for boxes, suitcases, tea-chests, canvases, assorted frames for bordering and for stretching canvasses, jars and pots filled with stiffened brushes and plastic sacs tied at the neck.

Nils stood for a few moments contemplating a couple of large, worn, matching holdalls before lifting one onto the nearest box and unfastening stiff straps and clasps. He pulled open the top and cursed under his breath when exercise books and surgical instruments were revealed. He had emptied some relics of his time spent at university into this bag on moving to the island, thinking perhaps he might study again to inform his article writing, but the veterinary profession had moved on and left him behind. He pushed away the opened bag impatiently.

He dragged forward the other holdall, hefted it onto a box and undid the top. It gaped open, revealing lacy underwear and high strappy sandals. He rummaged around until he found what he was looking for; a carved olive wood box inlaid with pearl. He carefully removed an amber necklace strung on silver wire, lifted it twined between his fingers, turned it so it gleamed faintly in the thin light then, pocketing it, he smiled a slow smile, fastened and replaced the bag beside the other and switched off the lantern. He left, locking the door and replacing the key on its high ledge.

CHAPTER 13
MEETINGS WITH GYPSIES

Anna and Maggie sat side by side on bar stools in the cocktail lounge of the Jacaranda Jardin hotel. The fortune teller had been delayed by an unforeseen accident on the road from Palma, which allowed them time to try the bartender's cocktail of the week.

'I can't believe they're still doing the Macarena,' said Anna, pausing to remove the tiny parasol from her drink as she watched the holidaymakers on the dance floor.

'They still do the Birdie Song in some places,' Maggie laughed, 'that reminds me; get back to what you were telling me about what happened the other day. If you've got over the thrushes, what happened after the castle?'

'Well,' said Anna, 'I haven't got to the best bit yet. When we arrived back in Palma, Jamil said he was taking me to meet some people. I said "yes" but we'd had a long day and I was hoping they weren't posh or anything because I was wilting a bit and it was getting late. Anyway, he drove to those streets behind the big new city-centre development.'

'What, the old tenements, behind the department store?' said Maggie.

'I thought it might be dangerous after dark but he parked that big car and we walked further in, to a building with lights on. There was no glass in the windows and the light was shining out from the upstairs floor. It seemed to be some sort of meeting place; I think it might have been an old theatre . . . teatro? Anyway we went inside, there was no door, up a narrow staircase and into a big room where there were lots of people and they looked like gypsies, you know?'

Maggie's eyes grew rounder.

'It was like a church meeting. Have you heard of the Bahá'is?

Maggie shook her head slowly from side to side. 'Are they some sort of sect?'

'It's a religion. Jamil says it began in Shiraz, in Persia, which is the place his family came from. It was started by someone whose name I can't remember . . . Bob . . . no that's not right.'

'Bob?' Maggie was incredulous.

'Anyway, they preach world peace through all the major religions getting together.'

'Sounds like a plan, but one that'll never happen.'

'Well, Jamil's given me a book to read; he's very serious.'

'So, what about the other people, the gypsies?'

'A lot of them crowded round Jamil. He said, "this is Anna. She's probably always been a Bahá'i and didn't know it". I liked that. It was a good way of breaking the ice. But they all talked in Spanish and Jamil gave money to some of the men.'

'Payment for something?' Maggie speculated. 'He did say he does business with the people he was taking you to meet, didn't he?'

'You must be right . . . I suppose. Jamil said it's required that the wealthier members in the community tithe part of their wealth, but handing it out personally in public seems an odd way to do it.'

'Didn't you feel a bit strange amongst them all?'

'Kind of, but they seemed friendly; I just couldn't understand any of them.'

'Then they did that sort of singing, you know, like gospel singing, standing up and swaying about, clapping hands. There didn't seem to be anyone in charge; the music was on a cassette.'

'Did anything else happen?'

'Well . . . Jamil left me for a few minutes with a woman called Lolly, I think that's short for Lolita; he went off with one of the men. He said Lolly could speak English but she couldn't. She called an old man over, I think he was called Gabriel, and I think he knew where I was living because he was talking about a caverna, you know, like taverna. That's a cave isn't it? But he couldn't really speak English either. He kept gesturing at me and going on about a ruby.'

'A ruby?' Maggie alternately nodded then shook her head as she followed Anna's reported sequence of events.

'Yes, maybe there's one hidden in the cave. What do you think? There was a dana or a dama; is that a lady? And something horrorizado. It sounded interesting but I can't remember any more. Does horrorizado mean horrible? Then Jamil came back and we left soon after and he drove me back to Terreno. It was a bit late.'

'A dama is a lady and I think horrorizado means

something like petrified in English. A very frightened lady perhaps?'

'Maybe, or maybe he was saying something was horrible, and what about a ruby?'

'Nils is horrible, you're a lady and you're going to find a ruby.'

Anna's laughter was interrupted by a voice coming from speakers above the bar. An announcement in English informed them the fortune teller had arrived and was setting up in a small salon off the main lounge area. She would receive clients in about ten minutes in the order of the number printed on the reverse of their tickets.

Anna and Maggie looked at theirs doubtfully. Printed on the reverse were the numbers one hundred and forty seven and one hundred and forty eight.

'Either she predicted a seriously busy evening tonight or she was part-way through a used book.' Maggie slid off her stool. 'Come on, we'd better head in the general direction and see how many others are there.'

They found a closed door with a notice printed on the back of a menu stuck to it with Blu-tack. A handful of hotel guests were seated in an adjacent corner drinking and chatting, their tickets in evidence on the tables in front of them.

'We may as well sit down.' Anna put her bag on the last unoccupied table and Maggie followed suit.

'What do you think she'll tell us?' said Anna. 'I'd love to know if my book will be a success.'

'Oh, the usual stuff; crossing water, meeting mysterious strangers. It's a bit late for predicting whether we'll have children. Perhaps I'm going to get divorced and you're going to get married. Do you think you and Nils will live happily ever after?'

Anna shrugged her shoulders.

'He's not a father figure is he Anna? Don't mind me asking, but he is quite a bit older and I know it's not all that long since you lost your parents. It wouldn't be unusual, even at our age. Tell me to mind my own business.'

'Well,' Anna grinned, 'mind your own business. I've always had a thing for older men. Nils is intriguing and sexy and he's good to me. When you take having children out of the equation, the body clock doesn't tick quite so loudly. Honestly Maggie, I'm happy.'

'Okay, that's that sorted out. I'll keep my fingers crossed for good predictions for your book; how is it coming along by the way?'

'I've just finished a complete first draft and sent it off to my agent; you remember, my friend Sue Greenwood. I've had a quick email from her and she loves my illustrations, especially the ones of the cave and the castle. I've been working really well since moving in with Nils. Everything seemed to come together like magic, even response times with my editor and publisher all seem to have speeded up.'

'Congratulations,' said Maggie raising her glass, 'and did everyone live happily ever after?'

'Of course. The dragon came down from the mountain. He knew the secret of which one of the carpets belonging to the prince was the magic flying carpet and knew how to activate it. Prince Jasper was able to fly into the night sky and turn off the stars so the sun could shine again. All the people were grateful to their prince and to the dragon for restoring justice and sunshine to their world. The wicked queen and the ogre were banished from the kingdom and the dragon returned to his cave but promised to come back again to punish any evil-doers.'

'Will the dragon be coming back?' asked Maggie.

'I'm not sure,' said Anna, 'but dragons are immortal aren't they? So who knows?'

Just then the door of the small salon opened and a woman, the wrong side of middle-age, wearing a colourful headscarf with small gold coins sewn around the edge and large hoop earrings put her head out. She looked around expectantly.

'Sorry to keep you all waiting but if number one hundred and forty seven is here, you're first.'

'Oh!' said Anna, standing up in surprise.

'It's because I bought the tickets a while ago,' said Maggie. 'Hope she's good; she's certainly dressed for the part,' she added in a low voice.

'What's her name?' Anna asked over her shoulder.

'Queenie Bishop.'

'What . . . like chess pieces?'

Maggie made a face and Anna followed Queenie into the room and closed the door behind them.

Queenie seated herself on a rattan peacock chair draped with an embroidered silk shawl. She invited Anna to sit opposite her on an upholstered hotel dining chair with a circular table between them. Behind Queenie, posters of strange astrological symbols and the twelve birth signs were tacked to the wall and behind Anna, just inside the door, was a table where an empty coffee machine and a disused computer sat side by side. The lighting was quite bright and there was no crystal ball.

'If you don't mind me asking, what kind of fortune teller are you?' Anna ventured.

'Of course I don't mind dear. You pays your money,' said Queenie briskly. 'I'm psychic, mainly. It runs in my family; Romany gypsies; go back generations. I give spiritual readings back home in England, the odd séance; do a bit of healing, that sort of thing. When I need a change of scene I come over to Mallorca for a holiday and do the English hotels; bit of a sun-worshipper, I am. I use cards to help with quick sessions.'

'You mean Tarot?' asked Anna.

'Oh no dear, that's just an elaborate game, that is. All that major and minor arcana stuff *and* they're supposed to be hand painted.' Queenie dismissed such trappings with derision. 'I don't need a crystal ball either, although I've a nice one at home, bought it off a white witch on a wet weekend on Preston market. Now let's get on shall we?' She placed a stack of ordinary looking playing cards on the table.

'It's not a full deck, eight cards from each of the four suites; the ace, king, queen, knave and numbers seven to ten. These cards are a bit different, they aren't reversible but they've got a top and a bottom, the images change slightly depending on which way up they are. You can pick four cards from each suite and turn them over whichever way you want. We'll do diamonds first, for the beginning of things.'

Queenie took the first eight red cards, spread them

across the table and watched Anna expectantly. Anna hesitantly turned over four of them.

‘Let’s see,’ said Queenie. ‘The king is very fair-skinned, possibly a white-haired man,’ Anna looked up and Queenie continued, ‘Is he in your life dear? He is a schemer who lets nothing stand in his way.’

‘Are you sure?’ asked Anna frowning slightly at the printed image in front of her.

‘The card is upside down,’ said Queenie simply. ‘He was involved with a fair haired woman but she was a flirt. The nine is also upside down and that signifies domestic wrangling; disagreement between lovers. Was that you dear or . . . before? Some of it clings to you, perhaps from where you’ve been; but it’s quite strong dear.’ Anna didn’t reply. ‘The ace is a letter; it could be an offer or proposal of some sort, that one’s difficult to read. We move on to the eight of diamonds; fate opens passages to ease the pathway of love. Good heavens, I’ve never seen such a clear view, something’s on your side in this one dear, you’re practically being propelled along.’

After a brief pause, Queenie laid out the hearts. ‘They represent the present.’

Anna turned over another four red cards and placed her hands back in her lap. Queenie studied her a little more closely.

‘The fair-haired queen is you, good. The ace says there’s been a removal of some sort. Have you moved house, dear?’ Without waiting for a reply she continued, ‘Oh, and the eight of hearts means thoughts of marriage... to a fair man.’ She studied Anna. ‘A little early yet but mark my words. Is this the same man dear? The ten upside down is an antidote to bad things; always useful. Do you need that, dear? You have worries but they will gradually pass. Do you want to ask me anything?' Anna shook her head.

'Well, clubs next. These are usually connected to the men in your life dear, as we look towards the future.'

Anna shifted her position, reminding herself that she didn't believe any of this. Half of the male population must be fair. Then she remembered that she was in Spain, which lowered the odds considerably. She turned the first four black cards over; a third ace, another king, a nine and an upside down ten. The ace was also upside down. Queenie glanced at her.

'Correspondence, tiresome I think, but it relates to coming into money, so, interesting but . . . rather hard to read again. Some things pass through clouds. Upside down means someone's happiness may be short-lived, but that doesn't necessarily mean it's yours dear; it could be a man close to you. This king is a dark man but you can probably trust him, follow your instincts. Nine represents an unexpected inheritance, it could be money acquired under a will and connected to a man.'

Anna thought of the garage which had already been indirectly inherited from her father but all the paperwork was still being completed. Spanish law was a tangle of red tape. Or was something else going to happen?

'Finally,' said Queenie, 'an upside down ten; always a sea voyage.'

'Who me, or a man?' asked Anna.

Queenie remained quiet for a few moments, putting a hand to her face, fingering her lips whilst seeming deep in thought. Her shoulders shook with a small shiver or shudder. She adjusted her scarf, cleared her throat and continued.

'There are journeys over the sea but not *on* the sea. There is no aeroplane but great distances are covered swiftly. This is a significant part of your reading but it can't be you.' She raised her eyes and studied Anna more closely than before. 'The clouds are quite thick.' After a few moments' silence, Queenie looked away, 'Let's get on. Just spades to do.' She spread the remaining eight cards. 'These cards point to the future, though mainly as a result of decisions taken in the past. Past, present and future, all these interact and overlap, dear.'

Anna turned over the last four black cards. A fourth ace, upside down, a knave, a seven and a nine.

'The knave is a medical student of some sort. Do you know anyone like that, dear?' Anna shook her head.

'Good,' said Queenie, 'because he has a very dark side to his character. The seven of spades means a resolve has been made. The fates are bringing together the past and the present to orchestrate retribution. You are part of it, but how it works is not revealed.' She paused to glance up at Anna then down at the table again.

'I see you are a writer, dear; that's interesting. The world needs storytellers; tellers of fables. Now, where was I? Ah, the nine is a bad omen; news of a death possibly, but where in time this occurs is not clear. It isn't your death, dear, don't be alarmed. However the cards point to the future so either it hasn't happened yet or perhaps the news of it is delayed somehow. The ace upside down is also news of a death. Well, people die all the time. All we know here is that this death touches you in some way. Everyone dies; we are all involved in the cycle of life.'

Queenie shrugged and leaning across the table, took Anna's hands in hers. She examined Anna's palms then sat back and regarded her thoughtfully before summing up with a strange warning.

***

The Jacaranda Jardin had a small public restaurant where Anna and Maggie had agreed to have a meal together after having their fortunes told. Anna saved a table until Maggie joined her.

'I need another drink,' said Maggie.

'Why, what did she say?' asked Anna.

'You first,' said Maggie, 'spill the beans.'

Anna took a gulp of her own drink before revealing what Queenie had told her, followed by her strange warning. 'She said she's sure I'm being haunted; something very old has found me. She's seen something similar once before but what's haunting me is much more powerful. It comes and goes. She said it won't hurt me but it will use me to achieve its own ends. I have to watch out for it.'

'What?!' Maggie exclaimed, causing a few other diners to turn and stare. 'Watch out for what?'

'That's just it,' said Anna, 'I've no idea. Listen to the science bit. Apparently, what we think we see and feel is created by our brains using special pattern-matching systems to build solid objects from random data hitting the backs of our eyeballs. Did you know that? I didn't. A lot of what's around gets filtered out because we haven't evolved far enough to see it yet. Queenie said we need to stare deeply, like into a 3D design, to see the image hidden in the background. Once your eyes adjust and you can see it, you wonder why you couldn't see it all along. In other words, just because we can't see things doesn't mean they're not there. Something could be creeping up on me now for all I know.'

The two friends stared at each other in silence for a few seconds before bursting into nervous laughter.

'She actually said she doesn't believe in it herself but there's a traditional Spanish folk healer called a curandero who's the only one who can treat mal puesto, that's a condition with symptoms from supernatural causes, and even though she doesn't believe in it, she said I could always try and find one of these healers.'

Anna looked over her shoulder and jumped violently as a waiter leaned towards her to offer a menu. He joined in the laughter, none of them knowing exactly what it was they were laughing at.

The waiter worked late, humouring the hotel's mainly British guests. His cousin, a taxi driver, drove home two women who'd clearly had a good night out.

Maggie went to bed, having enjoyed a very entertaining evening, and dreamed she was part of a swarthy skinned congregation chanting and clapping in a tenement block, hidden somewhere in the heart of the city.

Anna lay in bed, where she shared some of the fortune teller's insights with an extremely sceptical Nils before falling asleep.

***

She wandered where warm grasses waved and

whispered and bright blue harebells tinkled in the sunshine. Small creatures went about their business, creeping, crawling, buzzing and scratching, burrowing, basking and feeding.

CHAPTER 14
BIRTHDAY SURPRISES

Neighbouring diners performed showy social manoeuvres and complex mating rituals: pecking cheeks, fluttering hands, calling out to one another and to waiters for recognition and attention. The scented air was filled with voices, sounds of clinking glassware and cutlery, and the soft patter of numerous small fountains. Classically posed statues and gilded cages containing tiny calling birds added to the baroque surroundings. The extravaganza of exotic foliage was fronted by great baskets swathed in sumptuous fabrics which overflowed with tropical fruit like magnificent horns of plenty.

Nils had decided to celebrate Anna's birthday by taking her to a restaurant reputed to be one of the world's most romantic settings, Abaco, a preserved period house with an ancient courtyard and garden set behind Palma's Passeig des Born. The tables were set with candles, silverware, fresh flowers, linen napkins and appetisers of various Mallorcan delicacies. The dishes described on the menu were as sumptuous as the surroundings, causing Anna to declare that they would have to stay here very late to do everything justice, which was fine as she absolutely loved the place and if only she had visited here first she would have included a banqueting scene in her story.

‘So, include it in the next one.’ Nils’ attitude to her writing was nonchalant.

‘The next one’s going to be very different. I’m plotting a murder mystery for more adult readers set mainly on this island . . . in fact, you may be the inspiration for the intriguing male character,’ Anna added teasingly.

Nils regarded her with affectionate indulgence. ‘What is to be found on these islands has inspired many writers. For example, it is said that Spanish baroque, such as we have here around us, was unsurpassed anywhere in Europe as it embraced the traditions of both a medieval and a Moorish past. There are a great many examples here, especially in churches and cathedrals. We must travel, we must explore together. There is baroque music at the International Festival of Classical Music in Pollenca and also in Deia; we have missed them this summer; next year we will attend together.’

‘Next year?’ Anna smiled and squeezed his hand. She fingered the amber necklace lying warm against her skin. She had been completely surprised by it and declared it to be ‘absolutely beautiful’, just as Jane had predicted she would.

A few dinner guests passed by their table, strolling on through a bowered archway into the walled garden which was artfully illuminated and filled with a profusion of late summer flowers; neroli lilies, pelargoniums, roses and hibiscus.

***

The Dragon lingered in the small grove of ornamental orange trees. Baroque suited him; rooted

in a mournful Catholic past, it spoke of ancient tradition, power, fear and superstition. Dusty ossuaries of human remains related back to times when beings like himself were believed in and feared. In today's world, his power had not diminished; only the perception of it.

He moved further from the caged bird hanging nearest to him; the creature was becoming too agitated and was attracting too much attention to its location. He returned his own attention to the players in his game. The amber necklace glowed. The flaws in the irregularly shaped pieces told stories of the natural world which preceded the life of its present wearer by many human lifespans and would go on to outlive her indefinitely. Many humans would purchase ownership and it would grace many shades of human skin. For now it was a device, helping to first promote romance then foster suspicion between these two.

Nils' aura was glowing amber and scarlet, Anna's was all delicate yellow and warm pinks. The Dragon stretched his jaws in a sneer at the contrasts and jerky interplay between them; these two humans were completely incompatible, but humans could always surprise him. However, his interest only lay in furthering their short-term future, until his purpose was fulfilled. Nils' misdeeds must find him out, too much time had turned but now he was slowly, unwittingly facilitating his own fate.

The Dragon's plans had been thwarted with Eva but he would not fail with Anna.

He had worked to hurry along the completion of

Anna's childrens' story and was speeding up time in certain quarters to facilitate its progression towards publication. She must write her next one before he could be satisfied his work was done.

In the meantime, more birds were becoming agitated, picking up distress signals from each other; the Dragon made his departure; the songbirds settled on their perches and the orange trees exuded their delicate fragrance, masking other scents.

***

Nils and Anna sneaked a kiss across the corner of their table. Nils decided the time was right for something he wanted to tell her.

'You are comfortable in my home, are you not?'

'Yes, you know I am. Why?'

'I have a need to go away on business and for you to accompany me would not be suitable.'

'Oh, where are you going?'

'I must visit my brother in Copenhagen, over family matters, but I am afraid there is what is commonly called bad blood between us; we no longer speak. Our business concerns disposal of the family farmlands. It is complicated, so I will go alone and return after two or three days. I will keep in contact by phone and you will be able to reach me.'

Anna nodded her head, 'I understand. When are you going?'

'In a few weeks; the third weekend in October.' Nils felt the resurgence of long-buried memories. 'It is also a time when towns in Jutland celebrate with apple festivals. There has been no one to gather crops on the old farm for many years. The trees grow crooked from the west wind but the fruit was always good.'

'Does no one live there? No one at all?'

'No. The land belongs still to me and to Erik also.'

Nils refocused his mind on the present and saw a man on the edge of a small social group was standing with his back to them, too close up behind Anna's seat. He had been poised and quiet but now the sound of his voice and expansive gestures betrayed him to be the Englishman, Mike Redmayne. Nils was about to react by suggesting he and Anna leave their table for a stroll in the gardens but Red's group were already drifting, clutching empty glasses, in the direction of the bar. Anna had recently terminated her arrangement with Red and appeared to be unaware of his presence in the restaurant.

Nils was reminded of another associate of Anna's he had been wanting to discuss with her. She was presently relaxed, sipping a peach liqueur, listening to the notes of a dreamy nocturne drifting from the piano.

'You have made no further arrangements to see the carpet seller from the Gallerias?'

'Jamil? No, I said I wouldn't. That last trip was really useful for my book but I told him I wasn't available any more. He said I could let him know if I changed my mind.'

'I have reason to believe he trades in goods mis-appropriated from churches and religious institutions, perhaps in the countryside or more probably on the mainland. He colludes to redistribute the wealth of the Catholic Church.'

'You mean a sort of philanthropist?'

Nils gave a half smile and slowly shook his head,

'Your naivety is endearing, but no. The strategy is simple; it is that of hiding in plain sight the plundered goods. Even his parrot is evidence, with its ecclesiastical vocabulary. Men of the cloth do not shop in his emporium, it is only the island's wealthy homeowners who crave such trappings of wealth; perhaps those of a different religion. I believe such a process is known to the authorities in your country as a washing operation, doing laundry.'

'Money laundering? You mean he robs the rich and gives it to the poor?'

'Indeed. You sound shocked. The so-called poor do the robbing and he gives them money for it. He thinks he is some kind of demigod. The English have such a folk hero have they not? I have read of Robin of Loxley.'

'Robin Hood?'

'Yes, just so.'

'He was a real person.'

'I did not say I approve or disapprove but the Spanish police would hold a most different view. You should make your break with this seller of antiquities a permanent one. In this way, you do not invite trouble to our door.'

'I will, I promise. I can't believe it. Well . . . maybe I can, actually. Oh dear. Well at least I've never bought anything from him.'

'We need not discuss the matter further and I think we should walk around the gardens. You look most attractive and we must show off your necklace.'

Nils rose and leaned towards Anna to pull back her chair. His eyes slipped over the amber necklace and he pictured lightly freckled, creamy skin, a warm and generous cleavage, inviting in an unexpected way. It dawned on him for the first time that Jane reminded him of his mother. Certainly an odd connection, and one which momentarily disconcerted him.

***

He and Erik were running into the farmhouse kitchen, their bare feet and fingers blue from the juice of berries growing amongst the heather where they had played all day. Their mother gathered them both up in strong arms. She smelled of the milking shed. Her fair hair was plaited and coiled neatly about her head, a gay little red cotton scarf tied in it somehow. Under her pinafore she wore a starched blouse, the sleeves rolled back over her freckled arms. She carried both boys to a bath of warm water, leaning over to settle them at either end so that four dirty boy's knees stuck up in the middle. The memory was pleasant, warm and comforting; he shook it away.

***

The here and now had become more enjoyable since meeting Anna; he had a physical relationship again and plans for a shared future. He was going to be able to put the past behind him.

Before strolling, he made a visit to the gentlemen's facilities on the first floor, so he did not witness the hand that gripped Anna's arm, the surprise in her eyes, followed by a fleeting smile of recognition which was quickly replaced by a frown and a pulling away; a brief exchange of words, aggressive on Red's part, defensive on Anna's. He also failed to notice anxiety in her eyes as she searched the room before relaxing with relief at his approach. She smiled and gripped his hand possessively.

After leaving the restaurant, they strolled along the tree-lined Born together. The buildings on either side of the avenue, above the shop fronts, stood tall and timeless. Wrought iron balconies, huge hanging lamps, doors and windows decorated with ornate mouldings, frescos and canopies; the whole, a jumble of ancient and modern architecture jostling for space. Regular patrons and sightseers alike were becalmed, spilled over café chairs and tables placed outside in the balmy night air.

Anna talked of how she had only been there in the daytime before, noting shop window displays, busy pavements and wilting queues for buses, never imagining it could be so romantic. She noticed for the first time that the bowl of the old stone fountain was upheld on the backs of four turtles, just like the coffee table in the apartment of someone she had once done housework for. Did Nils know of anything in the island's folklore which referred to turtles; or were they tortoises? He didn't, but he guessed the owners of such a coffee table had probably been Max and Sylvia Gold.

As they sat on one of the curved stone benches, here and there in the shadows around them young lovers blended their shadows together. A fairy necklace of lights looped through the darkness overhead from the branches of one silvery plane tree to another and the night air seemed to be filled with gentle rustlings and whisperings.

Nils' and Anna's conversation turned again to Nils' proposed trip to Copenhagen. Anna was curious about the farm.

'Why are you selling it now? Why didn't you sell it a long time ago?'

'The land belongs to both of us, Erik and myself. It is complicated.'

'Why didn't you sell it when you left? Erik lives in Copenhagen, doesn't he?'

'Yes, Erik set up his veterinary practice in Copenhagen. I believe he does very well. I worked hard on the land but I have told you how farming in Denmark changed. I did not know how to leave. Then I became unwell one summer and came to this island to become better. Time passed by. I found the property where I now live to be for sale for a very low sum of money. No one was interested, it had been overlooked for years and was in great disrepair, not considered habitable. The family who owned it had left the island some time before; a time when tourism was only beginning. About the same time I met Holger among the Scandinavian community and we talked of opening a restaurant. Working the farm held no more attraction for me. I was drawn to the life this island had to offer. My brother Erik had his life and was not in need of money. I had considered tenant farmers but this had its problems and did not happen, and the land quickly fell fallow. Decisions were delayed and communication between me and Erik became irregular as my life here became settled, decided. I made my home and Holger and I opened our restaurant.'

Anna's listened intently with a faraway look in her eyes, as her imagination conjured scenes from Nils' earlier years.

'After some time Erik would come to visit. The cave held a fascination for him also. He had helped me with some renovations. Also we would cycle together as in our youth in Jutland. The farm held all our memories. We did not seek to turn it into capital and besides, either of us could always go back there.'

'Did you ever go back?'

Nils shook his head slowly. 'No. My life is here, and now I have reason to be even more happy and to make a life for us together for the future. But now Erik has made contact again. He needs money to extend his practice and has no sentiment over the past. With money from the farmland, it is true, I also could increase the comfort of our lives.'

'What a shame. The old farm sounds fascinating and romantic,' said Anna.

Nils grunted and rose to his feet, offering her his arm. He contemplated his forthcoming trip with mixed emotions of anger, resentment and bitterness. There was much of which he did not wish to be reminded. He foresaw that personal scores would not be settled and neither could he see that this visit would bring any satisfaction or closure to him.

His heart was loyal to his homeland, but so much about it had betrayed him, disappointed him. He would not go to Jutland, the land that had made him strong, the land whose lakes, peat bogs and central heaths had been transformed by his ancestors, farmed by his forefathers and sheltered their remains.

His thoughts ran with the winds up the jagged coastline. The salt air thrashing the sharp blue-green blades of grasses which covered the grave mounds of Viking chieftains; everything the colour of sea and shifting sand. The ghosts which called him back had grown pale and cold. The soft sweetness of the summers and the fertility of the land had lost their power over him, spoiling like frozen food under the Mediterranean sun.

So, the farm was to be no more; well it could take its memories with it and be damned. He would visit Erik in Copenhagen, come to agreement with him, sign documents, do whatever was required and return to his life in Mallorca and to Anna as quickly as possible.

CHAPTER 15
REVELATIONS AND A BEE

Jane doodled the usual Viking helmet, a stone-age axe, a cow, and what might have been a banana.

'You're so predictable.' Anna confiscated the pot of crayons, placing it out of reach on the next table. She and Jane were enjoying an ice cold lager and late lunchtime tapas in Dali's when conversation turned inevitably to Nils and his planned business trip.

'Have you ever seen any pictures of the farm?' asked Jane.

'No, he doesn't seem to have any mementoes of his earlier life at all; no photos of family, nothing.'

'Strange . . . Does he have a great big box of Lego bricks somewhere? I bet it's put away in the storeroom. Anna, have you ever seen inside that storeroom?'

'No. He did admit some old things, art materials, belonging to Eva were put away in there. The rent lapsed on her studio apartment in Palma so the owner wanted it cleared out.'

'Speaking of the mysteriously absent Eva, let's have another look at her picture. Is it still in your bag?'

Anna slipped her fingers down inside a flat pocket in the bags lining and brought out the folded news-paper article reporting Eva's disappearance. She laid it open on the table and she and Jane studied it in silence before Jane slowly raised her eyes and Anna's hand went nervously to her throat. The unique size and shape of the individual pieces of amber strung on their silver wire told an indisputable truth; Eva and Anna were each wearing the same necklace.

'Right,' said Jane, 'that settles it. There's a mystery here. Just how much stuff did Eva leave behind and how can he be so sure she won't be coming back? How come everything to do with her is so secret? He's hiding something, Anna, and he's hiding it in that cave.'

Anna carefully unclasped the necklace and placed it gently on the table beside the photograph of Eva. 'What about the bats?' she asked weakly.

'Bats, my eye. He'll be telling you next they're *vampire* bats. When did you say he was going away?'

'The third weekend in October.'

'I'm coming over. I'd love to see this cave-house . . . and I promise not to bring my camera, or my special reporter's notebook.'

'Okay.' Anna was a little dubious, then she recalled the previous evening. 'Actually, I haven't told you yet, but Red's threatened to call. He wants to catch me on my own and I'm not sure what to do. I don't want Nils to know and I don't want any trouble.'

'I thought you weren't going round to his apartment anymore.'

'I'm not, but he's not very happy about it. He caught me when we were in Abaco's the other night, said he'd overheard about Nils being away and to expect a visit from him. I think he knows about something or he's looking for something, but I don't know what. I know he was doing business with Max and Sylvia Gold round about the time they were trying to buy the cave-house for silly sums of money. He was annoyed not to have had the opportunity to look inside the lock-up garage, you know, when I got Eli to open it for me.'

'You're right, he's looking for something,' said Jane, 'now I'm definitely coming when Nils goes away; bats or no bats,' she added firmly.

'You always make me feel better.' Anna's shoulders relaxed. She put the newspaper cutting back in her bag then, after a moment's thought, carefully wrapped two paper napkins around the amber necklace and placed that in her bag with the cutting. Jane watched her thoughtfully before something came to mind.

'I was in here the day you went out with your carpet seller, and Nils stopped outside and came in for a coffee. I remembered one of Eva's drawings was on the back wall somewhere so I found it and gave it to him.'

'He didn't mention it,' said Anna, 'what was it a drawing of?'

'Just a garden, or a field with flowers in it. He didn't say anything, just put it in his pocket. Actually I'd forgotten, but it was a sketch of a painting Eva did for Zhu's salon, back when she was a regular client there. I think she and Zhu became quite friendly.'

'Can I see it sometime?' Anna felt as if her brain was doing a jigsaw puzzle without the picture on the box, but that if she could get it right it would tell her something.

'Come now if you like,' said Jane, 'I know Zhu's got a cancelled appointment in half an hour. I said I might pop in and have a quick coffee.'

'Don't you ever do any work?' said Anna.

Jane gathered her things together, put some money on the table and stood up. 'I'm out on an assignment and my phone needs topping up. Come on.'

They threaded their way through a network of backstreets, avoiding the city bustle, and arrived at a side entrance to the appropriately named Hotel Centro. Anna followed Jane along thickly carpeted corridors to the main foyer where, beside a room for left luggage, a frosted glass door was etched with the words; *Salon de Tratamiento Therapeutico*, Therapeutic Treatments, below which, half a dozen other languages drew attention to the hotel's cosmopolitan clientele. There was also a hairdressers with a nail-bar, and a flower and gift shop on the far side of the foyer. It was always busy, its revolving glass doors in almost perpetual motion as people passed back and forth between the parched streets and the soothing relief of efficient air-conditioning.

Anna had been here before and knew that the small pool containing koi carp, set into the floor in the hotel's reception area, ran underneath a wall to reappear inside the salon where Zhu worked. Zhu was one of three therapists practising a variety of disciplines who logged regular bookings and casual clients in a large diary on a small marble desk. The surroundings were clinical but luxuriously appointed and one arched window looked out onto the busy main street beneath great hanging baskets of geraniums, petunias and trailing lobelia.

Zhu was arranging some magazines on a low table and looked up in surprise as Jane and Anna entered.

'I didn't think you'd have time to come. Hello Anna, it's nice to see you.'

'I do actually have to be somewhere else,' said Jane, 'but Anna and I were discussing Eva Christiansen's art; you remember, your client who was reported missing; Nils' wife, or ex-wife. I remembered there's a painting in here and I've brought Anna to see it, if that's okay. Can I get us some coffee?'

Zhu nodded solemnly. 'I'll bring a tray from reception and the painting is over there.' She indicated a back wall above a shelving unit of bottles and jars and slipped out to order coffee.

Anna and Jane walked over to look more closely at the painting. It had been done in a very free style in what appeared to be mixed oil-based mediums in vibrant colours. Anna stared in silence, she was looking at a scene straight out of her dreams. Tall grasses, bending flower heads, the red barn with a green roof and bright rays of sunshine; a lovely scene. In fact the picture was titled underneath, *Field of Dreams*.

'It looks like a child did it,' said Jane with her head on one side. 'Picasso said "all children are artists but most of them grow out of it" . . . or something like that.'

'Do you like it?' Zhu had returned with two cappuccinos.

'Yes,' said Anna, 'are there any others?'

'Only the one in the apartment, but that one's different, it's a dragon.'

'A field of flowers and a dragon.' Anna sat down heavily on a low chair covered in chartreuse coloured velvet.

Zhu watched her, and Jane looked from one to the other. 'What?'

'Eva was anxious and stressed,' said Zhu, 'she couldn't sleep, she was having nightmares. As part of her therapy I suggested she paint her dreams.'

'They're my dreams,' said Anna, 'I've been having the same dreams.'

No one knew what to say next.

'Here, drink your coffee,' said Jane, 'I'm thinking.'

'I went to a fortune teller with Maggie, Queenie Bishop, she said I was being haunted. Maggie and I laughed about it but I'm beginning to wonder if there's something in it.'

'Zhu isn't comfortable around Nils and I know she used to worry about Eva,' said Jane. 'Neither of us want you to be harmed or hurt or unhappy. Something's wrong, Anna, and you know it is.' She turned to Zhu, 'Is it Eva, Zhu? Do you think she's dead?'

Zhu looked unhappy. 'I agree something is not right. Eva may be involved but I don't know. There is still a faint sense of her around Nils, but it is faded; gone away, like her. His aura is complicated.'

'Have we any more clues?' Jane asked.

'The gypsies,' said Anna faintly. Something was making her feel sick; perhaps it was the yellow-green colour of the chair's upholstery. Chartreuse was surely best in a glass.

'What gypsies?'

'It's a long story, but Jamil introduced me to some gypsies, they live in a community here in the city. One of them, an old man, tried to talk to me but he only spoke Spanish and mine's hopeless. His name was Gabriel and he went on about a cave and a ruby and a petrified lady and . . . oh, I wish my Spanish was better.'

'And just when were you going to tell me all this?' Jane looked aggrieved.

'Well … today, really. I just hadn't got round to it.'

'Did the old man Gabriel have a beret, like a Frenchman, and missing front teeth?' Zhu asked quietly.

'Yes, he did,' said Anna, 'do you know him?'

'I think I may know where he can be found.' The salon door opened causing Zhu to start and turn around. 'Good day, Mrs Harper. You're a little early for your appointment but I am free. Please take a seat. I will be with you in a moment.' She turned back to Jane, and to Anna who had jumped off her chair with a guilty expression. 'Do you know where the old tenements are?'

'Of course,' said Jane.

'At the far end, on a corner, is a little stone house with broken walls around. It used to be a shop of some sort with outbuildings behind. Gabriel Delgardo lives there with his donkey. Delgardo means the thin one. The donkey is Chico.'

'Thanks,' said Jane. She squeezed Zhu's hand, winked at her and turned to go.

'Thanks, 'bye,' said Anna and followed Jane out of the salon.

Mrs Harper looked them up and down and sniffed audibly. A red and gold carp broke the surface of its pool and slid back underneath the water with a gentle glooping noise.

Anna and Jane walked briskly away from the hotel and skirted the outer edges of the tenements towards the rear where Zhu had directed them.

Even though it was almost siesta time the bustle of the city's industry and commerce surrounded them on all sides. The tip of a tall crane peeped over the rooftops, dangling its load of concrete blocks high in the air. Sudden bursts from a pneumatic drill competed with a persistent car alarm and a joyful peal of bells from one of the many local churches.

Once inside the tall walls of the tenements there was an eerie quiet, the silence broken by muted sounds from their invisible occupants; a clash of pots and pans, the bark of a dog, the cry of a child. Anna was attempting to walk softly as the echo of their footsteps ricocheted between the buildings when the unmistakeable braying of a donkey came from somewhere nearby. She and Jane looked at each other, exclaiming triumphantly in unison, 'Chico!'

A detached building with unsafe-looking walls and half a roof sat on a corner plot of land. Fallen masonry and broken wooden pallets, all overgrown with weeds, paved the way to a straggling plot of land where a donkey was tethered, his panniers of tourist souvenirs on the ground beside him. On a chunk of concrete in the sketchy shade of a fig tree sat an old man wearing a beret and clenching a pipe in the space where his front teeth had once been. At first he showed no reaction to the approaching women, then as they came nearer he took the pipe out of his mouth and displayed a toothless grin in the direction of Anna.

She held out her hand. 'Hola Señor Delgardo, cómo estás?'

'Bien, bien,' the old man nodded vigorously and gripped her hand as she introduced Jane and explained with halting words and gestures that her friend would speak for her because her Spanish was better.

Jane began a conversation which Anna found impossible to follow, so she waited and stroked Chico's soft dusty ears. When she patted his neck a film of dust the same colour as his coat eddied around and landed back on his fur. She had primed Jane with the key words she had managed to remember and recognized them being used in the conversation. The old man became quite animated over one or two points, waving his pipe around in every direction.

When Jane's questions seemed to have all been answered, Gabrielle stood up and presented each of his visitors with a clay pipe from Chico's panniers. He poured water from a bottle into one and, raising it to his lips, blew through it to produce a gurgling whistling noise. With this ceremony complete he grasped each of their hands in turn and enthusiastically bestowed them good wishes before waving them away.

Around the first corner they both broke into fits of supressed giggles.

'Right,' said Anna as they walked, 'what was all that about? What have we learned? You seemed to get on very well.'

'Well,' said Jane, 'considering my Spanish is Castellano and your friend there spoke a mixture of old Mallorquín and Catalán, I may have put two and two together and got five, but here goes . . . He remembered you, and when your carpet seller first introduced you he had obviously explained where you lived. Some of the gypsy community know that property; probably they've squatted illegally around there in the past. Gabrielle definitely knew there was a cave somewhere. Some of them knew Eva Christiansen because she used one or two of the young girls as artist's models in their traditional outfits. Gabrielle referred to her as "el rubio" which just means the blonde one, so I think that was your ruby.'

'Oh, shame,' said Anna, 'carry on.'

'Well, he also talked about a lady who seemed to be in the cave; a very frightened lady. He seems to want you to see her; he got very excited about the whole thing. I got the idea that there's still a way down there from above but Gabrielle's never been. His grandson, Jesus I think, has been because he has a little dog which has got in more than once and Jesus went in after it and saw the lady. He seemed to be describing her as wrapped around or draped in a sheet or something and this is apparently very impressively done. But although he wants you to see this lady, she's a big secret and you mustn't talk about her. Whether or not you can talk *to* her is anyone's guess.'

The back of the hotel was coming into view.

'Anna, I'm worried about you. You know we have a spare room if you ever need to get away.'

'Did he say anything about bats?'

'For goodness sake forget the bats; they're a red herring . . . well you know what I mean. Can you find the key to the storeroom door?'

Anna hesitated. 'I know where it is, it dropped off a ledge the other day when I accidently flicked it with a towel. I was chasing a bee.'

Jane stared at her. 'A *bee*! You're unbelievable! Were you ever going to tell me?'

'I really love living there and Nils is the best thing

that's happened to me in ages. I don't want it all to fall apart. I want things to stay as they are.'

'I'm more worried about what might happen to you next.' Jane gave an exasperated sigh.

'Look, I really do have to go but I'm coming round that weekend Nils is away; in a couple of weeks, yes? Don't go exploring without me.'

'Yes,' said Anna, 'and no.'

'Hold the fort until then and look out for Red sneaking around. Phone me, text me, anything.'

Anna gave Jane a big hug. 'Thank you for absolutely everything. Thank Zhu as well. I don't know what I'd do without you.'

'Neither do I,' said Jane, 'and another thing, please stop doing creepy dreaming.'

'I'll try!' Anna gave a final wave and headed off towards the department store.

Jane set off at a very brisk pace in the other direction.

***

The Dragon's features contorted into a rictus grin. He scorned the gullibility of humans, their easy credence when faced with what they called coincidences, freak acts of nature, strokes of luck. The appearance of a large bumble bee uncharacteristically visiting a bathroom in a cave; it was all so easy, everything happened for a reason.

Anna would resolve her anxieties and settle with Nils, at least for the time being; the future he had planned was getting closer all the time.

CHAPTER 16
THE NIGHT OF THE STORM

A storm had been prowling around the island all day. The agitated air caused the rigging of the tall masts in the harbour to creak and rattle and grey oily-looking water to slap against the sides of the boats. It turned over the leaves of the rubber trees, lifted the rubbish on the pavements and emptied al fresco cafés. The horses drawing carriages along the main paseos trotted a little more smartly as if time were short, and people everywhere hurried about their business. Tourists spent their money in the bars of their hotels; not venturing outside, 'just in case'.

Local residents remained unruffled. Autumn was frequently a time of storms in the Balearics, when most of a whole year's rainfall was deposited, sometimes over just a few days. The Island of the Pines was waiting to soak up a sorely needed drink.

On the terrace of the cave-house, the liana vines rustled and a few drops of rain fell now and then as if in warning. The sea beyond was a cold steel blue with small white capped waves. Puccini had stayed in, sleeping on an old blanket under the table, and Tosca had chosen the centre of the high bed.

Nils had been gone three days, intending to return from Denmark tomorrow. He had left reluctantly, Anna thought, for a visit to family and long neglected roots. He had packed carelessly, seeming irritable and preoccupied. Perhaps he found the imminent sale of his childhood home upsetting, though he'd never suggested that to be the case. Holger had driven him to the airport, taking the car back to Mange Tak where he could keep an eye on it until Nils' return.

Anna had also been preoccupied, restlessly pacing, tidying up, re-arranging small items and then pacing some more. There were various emails requiring her attention but little work was done, and she had been checking the storeroom key was still on its high ledge two or three times a day. She had no desire to begin exploring in there on her own but this evening was when Jane was coming over and her heart kept jumping with nervous anticipation as a variety of possible outcomes played in her head.

It was also the evening Red was most likely to fulfil his threat of paying her a visit and she found herself hoping very hard that Jane arrived first. Jane's job as a journalist meant she was used to following trails into obscure places and she had dismissed Anna's detailed directions to the cave-house as being unnecessary.

Large drops of rainwater pattered on the terrace; the downpour could not hold off much longer. Anna slipped out, checked again that she had left the wrought-iron gate unlocked and hurried back inside. She was wondering whether to phone Jane when her friend's face appeared on the other side of the French windows, making her jump.

'Come in. I'm a nervous wreck. I'm so glad you're not Red.'

'So am I,' said Jane with feeling.

As Anna closed and locked the door, the gathering

force of the wind whipped a magazine she had left on the terrace up into the air and out over the parapet.

'What a night!' Jane put a powerful torch and her shoulder bag down on the table and collapsed onto a sofa. She looked all around her. 'Wow, what a place; bit different to your old apartment. It's like stepping inside someone's imagination or into a book.'

Anna poured them a glass of wine each and brought some sandwiches out of the fridge and put them on the small table; Jane eyed them mischievously.

'I suppose you know the Danes are famous for giving us bacon? Is that what you eat?'

'They also gave us Spam,' said Anna drily, 'and I've seen a tin in your kitchen.'

'Guilty as charged,' said Jane. 'Right, what's happening?'

'Well, Nils went away as planned, he's coming back sometime tomorrow. I don't feel comfortable going behind his back, but, as he's not keen to talk about things and I am getting uneasy, maybe I have to do some fact-finding of my own.'

'Good for you,' said Jane, 'we'll have these sandwiches and a quick glass of wine then you can show me round and end the tour in the bathroom. You've got the key for the storeroom?'

'Yes, it's still where I found it.'

'It did occur to me that if he was concealing anything incriminating or illegal he didn't bother to hide the key very safely.'

'Yes,' said Anna, 'I thought that, although it was rather a fluke that I found it.'

'Hmm…, 'said Jane, biting into a roll filled with *sobrasada* and sliced olives. 'Apart from the ramblings of Delgardo and his donkey and your fortune teller's forebodings, what do we actually know; how do we know it; what doesn't add up and what are we looking for? Also what do we think Red might be looking for?' She took a few thoughtful sips from her glass.

'You're making this sound so serious,' said Anna, 'you promise it's not going to be an article for the magazine?'

'Scouts honour,' said Jane, 'and pass the sandwiches; I didn't get time for lunch today.'

Heavy rain had begun to pelt the terrace. It hit the glass doors like hailstones. It thrashed the liana vines and beat down the hibiscus plants. Thunder rolled in the hills and the first trident of forked lightning split the sky. It illuminated the view from the terrace in monochrome. The gathering fury outside made the cave-house seem like a retreat, protected by tons of rock. Puccini twitched and whimpered in his sleep.

Anna clutched her glass more tightly and leaned forward in her seat. 'The Golds old correspondence in the garage gave away that, presumably as property developers, they wanted to buy this place very badly, offering completely unrealistic sums of money. The question is why? Nils wasn't prepared to negotiate at any price and warned them off; seems strange for someone with his practical mind.'

'Calculating mind,' offered Jane. 'You didn't tell me that . . . very interesting. So there's something here, or about this place, that made it worth buying to the Golds and worth keeping to himself to Nils. That must be what we're looking for and would also explain why Mike Redmayne's hanging around. He picked up clues from the Golds but he doesn't know the answer either. He's just hoping to stumble over something and couldn't snoop about while Nils was home.'

The treadle of the old sewing machine, now all covered by a sheet, emitted a loud ratcheting creak, caught in cross-draughts forcing their way in from the raging elements on the terrace.

Jane glanced round. 'God, Anna, this place is spooky.'

Anna had lit all the candles the way Nils normally did but tonight unusual draughts made them shiver nervously in their sconces. Their dribbling tallow made her think of waxy teardrops and their flickering flames caused animated shadows to dance high up the walls. She focused her mind on Jane's questions.

'The garage contents also gave us that old report about Eva going missing. We wouldn't have looked for something like that otherwise, but there seems to have been no follow up as to whether or not she was found. What happened to her and why didn't Nils carry on looking and why won't he talk about her? There's no evidence of her anywhere here.' Anna glanced around herself as if she might have missed some tell-tale sign of her predecessor.

'Apart from the fact that Nils gave you her necklace which must have been here somewhere,' said Jane drily. 'If you ask me, it's a jolly good job you opened that garage. Come on, let's have the guided tour.'

Anna stood and pushed aside the heavy drape across the entrance to the bedroom.

As she passed through, Jane stared at the huge Florentine mirror with its starry speckled edges. 'I feel as if you could walk straight through there to Narnia or down the rabbit hole.'

'Please don't try,' said Anna, 'it feels like the sort of night when anything could happen.'

Tosca uncurled in the hollow she had made on the bed, stretched and curled up again without opening her eyes.

In the bathroom, Jane looked around in fascination and focused on the door set into the wall. Anna stood on tiptoe and inched the key off its ledge. It landed on the tiled floor and she picked it up.

'Here goes.' She inserted it in the lock and turned it.

As she pushed the door forward, a slight draught was sucked through the cave from somewhere and extinguished the bedroom candles. Jane had her torch in her hand and she stepped forward into dense moist darkness.

The friends stood shoulder to shoulder, perfectly still. The beam of Jane's torch arched around them, creating an illusion of objects advancing out of blackness towards them, then receding back again.

Eva's abandoned art materials were evident nearby; easels, palettes, stretching frames and open boxes holding jam-jars full of paint brushes. There were a number of carelessly placed boxes and suitcases, fastened and strapped up. One grip-bag had been left open and, as the torch beam circled, Anna glanced inside and saw, glinting in the light, what looked like assorted surgical instruments. She experienced a ripple of fear as her memory made a small connection. What had Queenie Bishop said? 'The knave is a medical student of some sort. Do you know anyone like that dear because he has a very dark side to his character?' What else had Queenie said?

The torch beam moved on as Jane inched forward and Anna moved to keep up; past two bicycles, showing signs of rust and neglect; Anna thought of Nils and Erik enjoying cycling together before . . . what? There was a moment of shock when she gripped Jane's arm as the flashlight beam fell on the tailor's dummy which had, at some time, migrated from the dining area into the storeroom. It now had a twin as it faced a discarded mirror leaning against the opposite wall. Together, Anna and Jane stepped warily between them.

The floor further in was uneven but smooth, a polished black basalt, and the walls very rough. The space narrowed to little more than a passageway, no longer hewn by human hands but formed by nature. The friends stumbled in the darkness. They paused for breath and listened. They could still hear the dull rumble of distant thunder, although from which direction it was impossible to tell. The storm had been right overhead when they began their exploration. Now as they listened they heard another, unexpected sound.

'Is that ticking?' Anna asked uncertainly.

'That's what it sounds like.' Jane cocked her head, senses alert.

There was a faint rhythmical sound, like an old kitchen clock marking the passage of time in the darkness. The torch beam gave nothing away as the now empty passageway was veering sideways ahead.

'Is it bats?' Anna flexed her shoulders as a bead of perspiration trickled down her back.

'Yeah, they're going to explode,' said Jane.

Suddenly a loud noise like a smashing of glass came from somewhere behind them. Anna and Jane both cried out in shock, turning in the narrow space, hearts thudding and adrenalin pumping. A rush of air came towards them, accompanied by other muffled bangs and crashes. They each froze momentarily.

Anna envisaged Red breaking in under the influence of drink, or, the even worse case scenario of masonry crashing down from somewhere above. Could they be trapped up here by a landslide? She experienced the first flutterings of claustrophobic panic rising into her throat and heard the pulse of her own blood.

'It's the storm,' said Jane, 'it's blown the French windows in. Damn, we'll have to go back, it's causing damage.'

They stumbled back the way they had come, following the wavering light of the torch beam. Just in front of the door back into the bathroom the battery-powered lantern suspended from an overhang of rock was thrown into relief.

'Well, we've found that for next time,' said Jane breathlessly, propelling Anna through the door and across the bathroom.

Now the threat of the storm seemed all around. The timber frames surrounding the French windows were old and dry and one had finally cracked under the pressure of rainwater hitting it in furious squalls. The large pane had shattered on the floor and Anna saw it was the angry night, not Red, which had broken into the room.

Outside, the terrace ran with rivulets of water heading for the steps down to the alley to make their escape. Surfaces glistened fitfully as storm clouds hurried past the moon.

Anna took in the scenario in horror. The only thing she could think of large enough to at least partially cover the gap where the door had been was a very big parasol which was stored in a corner of the bedroom and could perhaps be wedged into the space. She ran to get it, shouting as she did so to Jane to move things further back into the room.

The faded canvas parasol was erected and jammed in the gap where the glass door had been. Anna and Jane began to gather together pieces of splintered glass and place them carefully into a large cardboard box, hastily emptied of its contents. When they had collected all they could see, Anna dragged the box of glass shards through the remaining glass door and onto the terrace, out of the way.

The rain had become light; the moon was looking down from a clear sky. Anna took a few steps forward to take in the unfamiliar sight of the city's rooftops shining, brightened and freshened by the downpour. From somewhere she could hear the gurgling of drains and from below, the splashing of tyres as late night traffic began to flow again along the main paseo. From every direction came pattering noises like the scuttering feet of small creatures teaming over the wet surfaces. Everything around her dripped and glittered like fractured glass.

She turned; the dark figure of a man was standing motionless in shadow, just inside the gate. She gave a small shriek of shock; Red had carried out his threat to pay a visit and now she couldn't even lock him out.

The figure moved, and moonlight fell across his features. Nils had returned a day earlier than planned. 'What is happening? Are you all right?'

'Oh, thank goodness. One of the doors has broken inwards with the rain, it's smashed and I didn't know what to do.' Jane appeared at the sound of voices. 'Jane was here keeping me company in the storm. I asked her to come.'

Nils took charge. 'Go inside, go inside. The door is old but I see nothing here that cannot be fixed.' He ushered Anna and Jane back inside, placed his large travelling bag on the floor and surveyed the damage.

'So, we will make hot chocolate. I will see Jane,' he gave her an inscrutable look, 'to her car, then we will all go to bed and in the morning I will fit a new door.' He kissed Anna on her cheek. 'Now sit, I will make the drink. The storm did not invade the kitchen.'

'Excuse me, I'm going to the bathroom.' While Nils' back was turned, Anna motioned to Jane that she would go and lock the storeroom door. Jane nodded and leaning across the kitchen worktop, engaged Nils in conversation about his trip.

Soon they were all seated amicably around the dining table clutching mugs of thick hot chocolate. Nils had an unexpected story to tell.

'I have news of a serious nature; news of a death.'

Anna and Jane exchanged glances.

'A death tonight, in the storm. I was lucky the plane landed before the storm broke. I took a taxi from the airport. I went to the restaurant for the car and then drove along the harbour front. My intention was to cut up into Terreno but it became necessary to park for shelter; the road was not safe. There was commotion on the quayside, lights flashing and figures of men in the rain. Then there were sirens and police. It was obvious some sort of accident had occurred.'

'Who was it who died?' Anna couldn't wait.

'The Englishman, Mike Redmayne.'

'What happened?' Jane's voice took on a professional tone.

'As the rain stopped I left the car and questioned a man who had come across the road from the scene. He said it was reported the Englishman had been drinking all afternoon in a bar over the road, before taking out his boat to test some repairs to the hull. He said the man was tonto, a fool. It is believed he tried to get back into the port just as the storm was breaking and was capsized. Visibility was very bad and the quayside slippery; by the time the security guards managed to haul him out of the water it was too late for him, and the boat was dashed against the harbour wall. They said it had the name of "Good Roger".'

Anna swallowed hard as nervous laughter threatened to escape.

Nils frowned.

Jane drained her mug and pushed her chair back. 'Sorry folks, if I hurry now, I might be first with a story.' She quickly checked the contents of her bag.

Anna gave her a fierce look. 'I thought you weren't bringing your special reporter's notebook.'

'I didn't,' Jane said in mock defence, 'this is just my ordinary one. It lives in my bag. I'll ring you tomorrow. Don't worry about anything.' She squeezed Anna's shoulder.

Nils rose to his feet to offer to escort Jane up the alleyway to where her car was parked, but Jane dismissed his offer with a brief handshake and switched on her flashlight.

'I'm going down the steps and I'll be fine, honestly. If I get a scoop I'll owe you a drink. Go to bed both of you, it's been a very strange night.' Then she was gone.

Nils inspected the canvas parasol, shrugged and put his arms round Anna. 'I have missed you more than you know. I am sorry about your Red but I have to say he will not be missed by many.'

Anna closed her eyes and leant against him, tired and drained. 'I've missed you too.'

'So, come to bed, it is late, and tomorrow I will talk to you about my trip.'

Later, as Nils slept, Anna lay half asleep in the cocoon of darkness and of Nils' arms. She fancied she saw the blurred image of some kind of beast passing through the mirror.

***

Pure white brittle snow and ice crusted silent surroundings, but the creature was not Aslan the lion; perhaps this wasn't Narnia. She drifted through a winter landscape of gracefully iced skeletons of trees, down to where smaller shrubs looked like delicate fans of coral, undulating under the sea. They made a soft sighing sound. One had snagged a limp straw hat

wound round with a grubby striped tie which streamed in the current. Anna kept still to listen; the sighing sounded like whispering and the sheet she seemed to be wrapped in was coming unwound and floating away. The water weighed down on her but she wasn't wet and was able to breathe. She weight she felt was sadness.

Her bare feet trod on frozen seaweed, slipped through spikey grasses, lots of flowering plants she couldn't identify; then she fell, everything cracking, crumbling and giving way beneath her. The space around her seemed filled with fruit, apples which rattled and rumbled past her into the void. She reached out for one but it disintegrated in her hand revealing squirming maggots at its core. She was still wearing her sheet but now it was torn and grubby and she felt distressed and panicky.

She was still following the blurred creature but if it wasn't Aslan, it definitely wasn't Alice's White Rabbit either; what was it? Something about it seemed familiar. If she could just catch up with it…

'I'm coming,' she shouted, 'wait!'

***

She sat up, but the surface of the Florentine mirror was dark and impermeable. She slid out of bed and went to the bathroom medicine cabinet for tablets to help her sleep. She stripped off her vest and knickers, everything clammy with perspiration, and washed the tablets down with a long drink of water from an empty coffee mug left on the back of the washbasin. She cautiously checked the store-room door was locked then, feeling acutely aware of her nakedness and the now missing door to the terrace, she hurriedly slipped back between the bedcovers and lay close against Nils, waiting for her body to relax again.

CHAPTER 17
AN EASY DEATH

Nils rose early. He had a vague memory of Anna having taken a sleeping pill halfway through the night to calm her nerves. She had been more than usually restive, calling out in an anxious voice which then became muffled and indistinct. Now she remained asleep.

He contacted a glazier in San Augustin. The man, known as Pellegrino, was Italian, an artisan who understood glass. He had proved fast and efficient when a restaurant window had been damaged some time ago. He also understood where the cave-house was and was prepared to begin work immediately using Nils' measurements. The door would be replaced before evening.

Nils breakfasted on the terrace, alone with his thoughts. Rapidly evaporating moisture caused rooftops across the city to sparkle in the sunlight. Gulls arced over the bay on rising thermals, reminding him of the disorderly clouds of gulls, rising and descending, marking the slow progress of the plough over regimented furrows of fertile ground.

Puccini had not yet made his way down from his hideaway in the ruins above, while Tosca sat silently beside a dead mouse which had ceased to be of much interest. A tiny gecko lay camouflaged on the wall above her head, catching the sun's rays.

Morning light picked out lingering pockets of rainwater in cavities in the brickwork and hollows on the ground. Waterlogged hibiscus flowers drooped over beds of sodden clay-coloured soil; behind them, here and there, small rivulets trickled down the craggy rock face like miniature waterfalls which disappeared from view.

As the sun climbed higher there was a damp earthy smell and little ghosts of steam rose and evaporated above the puddles. Nils' reflective mood turned to memories of far northern graveyards where, in winter, in the freezing air, twisting ghosts had seemed to rise and linger, conjured into being by heated rectangular metal plates laid to thaw the ground before fresh interments.

His father's name was etched on a wooden grave marker in a cemetery in Jutland, near the coast where he had grown up. After a lifetime of hard work, Jens Christiansen had left the world courtesy of a particularly aggressive form of cancer.

The old church where Jens had worshipped in his youth was built of granite to withstand the salted air and the capricious sea. It was a bleak environment where once, long, long ago, freshly caught fish had hung on regiments of drying racks. Now only the church bell hung heavily from an oaken crossbeam and the cemetery was invaded by harsh blades of the lyme grass which clung to the ever-moving carpet of windblown sand cover. It was as if the grave mounds themselves moved slightly, slowly, eastwards. This was not an environment to which Nils had wished to commit his mother.

He recalled her face as she approached the end of her

life; the quandary and decision-making he'd faced alone had haunted him ever since. He had watched her suffer the creeping confusion of dementia, wanting only for her to be calm and safe and, when the time came, an easy death.

He favoured the Swedish practice of promession, quick freezing a body in liquid nitrogen until it shattered; he considered this practice to be eco-friendly, clean and practical and somehow kinder than cremation. Unfortunately it was also prohibitively expensive and not widely available.

Death of course lurked around every corner on farms and country people were known to sometimes defy laws and conventions by laying their loved ones to rest in the forests in woodland graves under the protective canopy of the great beech trees. Little grew in such dense shade; perhaps ferns, bluebells or foxgloves, and the floor of the forest was quiet, inhabited only by small shy creatures living secret lives. The trees would stand guard for a hundred years and ancient beliefs promised that the dead would make their contribution to the Earth's fertility, perpetuating the cycle of life.

Puccini got up from beside Nils' feet and pattered towards Anna, who had appeared in the space where the door had been.

'You should have woken me.'

'Oh, good morning. You needed to sleep and I had things to do.'

'I want to hear all about your trip. Did you enjoy it? How was Erik? Have you sorted everything out?' She sat beside him on her favourite seat, an old basket chair, misshapen and weathered. She was barefooted, wearing an oversized grey t-shirt and holding a large glass of orange juice.

'Would you like some?'

Nils shook his head. 'It was not a trip to be enjoyed, but successful in the resolution of affairs. There is a buyer for the farmland. It is to become a pig-farm.' After a pause during which he shook off an unwelcome vision of pigs rooting for the truffles which proliferated beneath the surface of the ground under the beech canopy, he added, 'Erik appears well, thank you; Eva is well also, she is pregnant.'

'Eva! You've seen her?'

'Of course, yes, Eva. Where did you think she was all this time?'

'I don't know. I didn't really think anything and you never said . . . You reported her missing.'

'How do you know that? Oh, I suppose that your reporter friend is a good source of such information.'

'No, actually.' Anna was defensive. 'I read about it in an old magazine. But what happened?'

'She and I did not work out so well and then when Erik visited here he was the favoured one. After he left, Eva followed him without the courtesy of an explanation or a discussion. My wife left all her belongings behind, both here and in her studio, and so I believed her missing; I made a report. When I learned the truth from my brother, I felt it was no one else's business. The Spanish police were not looking for her anyway; they are useless.

You look shocked, yes, my brother and my wife. So, you see now why I do not speak of her; she is dead to me. My brother says he is sorry, well, what shall I do with his sorrow, his guilt? How shall I now be an uncle? It is a burden we both must bear.'

Anna took his hand in one of hers. 'I'm so sorry, how awful. I never guessed. Oh dear, I really am sorry.'

'Please do not be. I have signed the necessary papers and a divorce will be finalised before the child is born. Eva will marry Erik and I will be free to re-marry, should the lady in my life feel the same. The past is past and the future is ours; be happy.'

Nils' expression softened, and releasing his hand, he leant over, took Anna's face in both of his hands and kissed her. 'You are my lady.'

Anna snuggled up to him and leant her head on his shoulder. 'Tell me about Copenhagen then. We could visit some time without seeing Erik or Eva.'

'I had no wish to visit Jutland or the farm but Copenhagen is, in the words of the song, wonderful. You would like it, I think. I must say of Erik that he made a good choice for his practice and for his home.'

A shout came from the alleyway and Nils jumped up to admit Pellegrino and his young helper as they struggled with a heavy plate of glass.

Anna returned to the interior where Nils could hear her talking on her phone. She was followed faithfully by Puccini, who sensed that breakfast might be on offer.

Nils had put off making the revelations concerning Erik and Eva for as long as possible. His male pride and his feelings had been deeply wounded by their actions and his anger had been explosive. Now time had passed, the cat was, as the English said, out of the bag; he felt better, he would move forwards.

So, Eva had become pregnant; well what was that supposed to prove? Although it was true he had believed that a problem such as infertility must surely reside within the female and not with a man such as himself.

He had recently read with interest, but no real surprise, of Denmark's booming artificial insemination industry. Danish sperm was collected at a facility in Arhus, Denmark's second largest city, and exported around the world. It was especially popular in territories once conquered by Vikings. In such areas the prospective parents hoped for tall blond children who would grow to resemble themselves, perpetuating the ancient cultural fusion. Ironic to consider how people now craved more of what their ancestors had fought to the death not to have forced upon them.

However, a family was anyway a burden and an expense and something Nils told himself he no longer desired. Erik had left parenthood late in life but it was something Eva had always wanted and now she had her dream; one which had severed sibling bonds forever and precipitated the sale of the family farmlands.

Enlightened times plus Nils' own studies had made him more aware that the very farming practices which had ruled his father's life might have had more than a hand in the cancer which hastened his death. As farmers fed their animals and sowed their fields, introducing a growing cocktail of harmful chemicals into the land, so the Grim Reaper reaped.

Meanwhile, Nils' interest in cultivating indigenous plant species for food had become more absorbing, leading him further and further away from animal husbandry. By the time his father, a worn out old man who did not deserve to suffer, lay dying, he had learned that poppies, which in summer painted the fields and embankments a vibrant living red, produced seed heads used in the production of morphine. Also, around the farm out-buildings, the tall flowering spires of bright yellow mulleins produced seeds which were an effective narcotic. But the berries of henbane, atropha belladonna, which he had discovered growing on the sand dunes, contained the most powerful drug.

So Jens Christiansen's final journey was accelerated in the arms of his elder son.

Nils rarely thought of these events now and had never visited his father's grave in its remote and depressing environs.

He had visited his mother's woodland grave many times in the past, in summer, resting himself on the moss of a tree trunk, fallen where the trifoliate leaves of wood sorrel represented the holy trinity and the tiny white flowers of wood anemones trembled in constant agitation. This forest glade was a favourite boyhood haunt where he trod again his secret pathways; in winter, his stout hiking boots striding out over fallen branches which lay brittle and blanched, dressed in their filigree of lichen; delicate lace-like strips and small natural sponges which clung, bone coloured, silver and sea green.

The dementia which in his mother's case had proved to be the early stages of Alzheimer's disease had been slow and cruel. Patterned floor coverings and uneven surfaces were interpreted as holes underfoot which turned even the safest environment into something perilous. Everything frightened and bewildered her and she became a danger to herself in a world she could no longer comprehend.

Nils had to work the farm, and the strain of keeping his mother, who sometimes didn't recognise him, safe and tranquillised through long days and sleepless nights became too heavy a burden to bear. With his father gone and little in the way of savings or insurance to fund extra hired help, he witnessed his mother's distress grow daily. Erik was selfishly building a successful practice in Copenhagen and did not fully grasp the extent of the problems back on the isolated farm.

Nils knew his mother was suffering a condition which could only be terminal and having successfully helped his father, he would now do the same for her. To act sooner rather than later made sense. He hardened his heart and turned again to his plant studies, seeking a route to an easy death.

He read that a substance called galantamine, derived from daffodils, was being used in the treatment of Alzheimer's; too late to experiment with that. He decided the humble foxglove was the answer to all their problems as it closely replicated many of the symptoms from which his mother already suffered, headaches, fatigue, weakness, disorientation, confusion and visual disturbances. He became confident a large dose of digoxin, correctly sourced, would intensify these and bring closure. The vomiting had been distressing but was mercifully brief.

All these and other memories chased him, ambushed him and sometimes haunted his dreams. Perhaps now that the farm was sold his mind would be more free.

***

The Dragon had been unconnected to the deaths

of each of Nils' parents but in the light of further events, he viewed them in flashback. He saw a hardworking family who had toiled on their farm for small rewards, but there was something bad, maybe a throwback to the old days, something locked in the genes but unacceptable now.

The ancestors of Jens Christiansen had been Vikings, men with their own codes of honour, men who were capable of earning more in one trading expedition than Jens earned in a lifetime. In the markets of Constantinople they bartered Baltic amber, walrus ivory, the pelts of small mammals and Anglo Saxon slaves from the counties of Northumbria, Mercia, East Anglia and Wessex, returning home with cargos of precious silk. Jens had not been much of a reader and had known little of them.

The Dragon had witnessed those exciting times evolve into something more civilised but in his untamed heart he mourned the passing of the old ways.

But he was a mere servant of fate, sent forth from another dimension, his purpose to make connections, close circles, nudge the moving finger, the one which writes and having writ moves on.

He had invaded Nils' psyche on the day when the human soul was in torment. The day on which Nils travelled alone to the edge of the warring seas at Skagen to give vent to his emotions against the thunder of the waters. There the mortal shed a pale shade of his youth and former self and on leaving, took with him an ancient avenger.

The Dragon had begun to influence Eva's painting

but his timing had been out and Eva had unexpectedly left the scene to begin a new life. However, the artist in Nils' life had been replaced with a writer and what could be better? One way or another, Nils would unconsciously engineer his own downfall. The Dragon knew fate offered alternatives but no escape route.

***

Nils attempted to assist Pellegrino and his young helper but received a clear message that they preferred to work unaided. A great deal of sawing and hammering was taking place so he suggested Anna dressed and accompanied him up the alleyway to the nearest bar for a late breakfast. She agreed, and soon they were sitting at one of the small aluminium tables beneath the weathered awning enjoying bocadillos filled with spicy chorizo sausage and drinking large tazas of hot coffee.

Behind them, in a corner of the bar, a Spanish newsreader babbled incessantly as pictures flashed across the television screen. In front of the bar's stretch of pavement, early traffic passed sporadically. The early morning air was energised with the scent of pine sap combined with ozone, carbon monoxide, coffee, liquors and while he served them, the bar owner's cigarillos.

Anna asked again about Copenhagen.

'I've seen pictures of the canals and the beautiful harbour in the town centre and I love the way the buildings are painted different colours; just like in a fairy tale. It would be a very romantic place to go for a birthday or anniversary.'

'Indeed, yes. As you know, my time studying was spent there at the Royal Veterinary and Agricultural

University. Not much has changed, but it is become very fashionable. Still everyone rides bicycles, they can carry much shopping, even passengers. It is a fascinating sight. Perhaps we will have a special celebration next year. When I am legally free I will ask you a question.'

Their eyes met, Anna's cheeks coloured and her gaze slipped downwards. Nils understood this to be an unspoken acceptance of the proposal he intended to make once the legalities surrounding his marriage to Eva were resolved.

'For now I must ask you a different question, but it is awkward. You and Jane, you are very good friends?'

Anna smiled. 'I know why you're asking and please don't! I've known Jane and Zhu ever since I came to the island. They are a very settled, well balanced couple and Jane is just a good friend who has never said or done anything to embarrass me or make me feel uncomfortable. She's intelligent and good company. Does that answer your question?'

Nils pursed his lips then smiled his half smile. 'I suppose so. Then we too will practice the Danish art of *hoo-ga.*'

'What on earth's that?'

'The word is spelled *h-y-g-g-e* in Danish and the translation is, "the art of cosy tranquillity".'

'Oh, all right, that sounds lovely.'

After a pause, Anna asked, 'I read the other day that Copenhagen has more Michelin stars per head than any other European city. Is that the sort of food you serve at Mange Tak?'

'Not exactly; typical Nordic cuisine has, like so much,

been hijacked by fashion and extortionate prices. However, the restaurant which has become most well-known, Noma, features foraged food and I applaud them for that. As you know, I have a great interest in utilising simple indigenous plants for nutrition and also medication of the human body. Do you know the saying that many men lie in their grave beside the plant that could have saved their life?'

Anna shook her head. 'I'd rather not think about dead people.'

CHAPTER 18
A PETRIFIED LADY

The large fan still droned in its corner, causing a plastic air-vent to flap uselessly beside it. The wall clock with a tick like a metronome marked the passing minutes and the same rubber plant still clung to life in its tub of dry earth in front of blinds closed against the glare of low winter sunshine.

Anna sat on a white plastic chair, once again waiting for an audience with Señor Martínez, who was the only connection she had to her evacuated apartment block. She waited patiently for the first ten minutes then she waited impatiently while the receptionist first busied herself on a keyboard then chattered excitedly on her mobile phone, all the time casting sideways glances to see whether or not the Englishwoman was listening to her private conversation.

No one departed the inner office and after twenty minutes, Señor Martínez became free to see Anna. She had made an appointment to enquire about the situation regarding the aluminosis; what, if anything, had been decided and what was to be done?

Señor Martínez seemed irritated by her presence. Hadn't she received the notice he had sent to everyone concerned? Perhaps the Spanish postal services had been unable to find the address her gentleman friend had given. No matter; the news was good. The aluminosis had been confirmed as being a very bad case; of course the building was old and were his advice to have been sought, he would not have advised anyone to have bought such a property. But the English in any case always shunned advice in such matters. However, a ruling had been passed that, with due consideration for its age, the building was to be condemned and the residents were to receive a modest sum in compensation.

Such a payment was not guaranteed in all similar circumstances and Anna was to consider herself fortunate. Furthermore, Anna's payment was to include a small amount for the garage.

Señor Martínez delivered this last piece of information, drumming his fingers on the desk and hesitating before revealing that he had tried and failed to contact Señora Gold through her bank and thus been forced to concede that the lock-ups inclusion in Anna's deeds must be correct. So, she could expect a sum of money, he was not sure how much, to be paid to her shortly, at which time she would be required to call again and sign the necessary paperwork. He noted her new postal address, her mobile phone number and Nils' landline number, then rose from his seat to signal that their meeting had reached its conclusion.

'If there is nothing else Señora, good afternoon.'

'Señorita, and good afternoon Señor Martínez.' Anna briefly shook his outstretched hand and left the office in good spirits, reflecting that whatever compensation she received would be her parents' final legacy to her. It may not be sufficient to buy another apartment but while it sat in the bank it would make her feel more secure. Importantly, it also offered increased independence of Nils' hospitality, should the need ever arise.

The two of them now had an unspoken understanding that Nils planned to propose they made their partnership permanent with marriage as soon as he was divorced from Eva. How did she feel about that? On most days she anticipated her answer to be a 'yes'. She firmly believed she and Nils were in love with each other. Just occasionally, she wavered a little and was thankful for more time to examine her feelings.

She asked herself what caused her to hesitate. The age difference didn't bother her. The relatively short time they'd known each other didn't bother her. Their backgrounds were different and their earlier lives had been lived far apart but they still felt compatible. The only thing she could think of was a vague lingering feeling that Nils was hiding something. Was there something sinister in the depths of the cave, or were she and her friends behaving like silly schoolgirls?

The morning after the storm she had gone inside and phoned Jane to ask whether she'd got home safely and to share the information regarding Eva. Jane was already at her desk and received the news in complete amazement.

'Well, we didn't guess that, did we? Can we print something?'

'No, please don't. He doesn't want people to know. That's why he didn't tell me sooner. I suppose he's embarrassed and anyway, people will have forgotten the original article by now.'

'Okay,' Jane was reluctant. 'You know Zhu didn't

think anything bad had necessarily happened to Eva; she just thought Nils was capable of something and Eva had gone because she was frightened. I still think he's got something to hide. I'd still like to know what's at the back of that cave. Wouldn't you?'

'Maybe . . . I don't know. But thank goodness for the storm, otherwise he'd have returned and caught us looking.'

'You see, you shouldn't feel like that. It's your home now. Anna, are you a bit frightened of him? Tell the truth.'

'Of course not, don't be silly.' Anna looked over her shoulder but Nils was still outside on the terrace. She could hear him talking to Pellegrino. 'I'll ask him to walk me right through to the end of it. Will that satisfy you?'

'He likes opera, doesn't he?'

'Yes, what's that got to do with anything?'

'Have you heard of one called Bluebeard's Castle?'

'No, why.'

'Bluebeard is a lonely man who brings his new bride home to his castle but won't reveal his past. His new wife makes him unlock all the castle doors. Behind them are other wives and lots of blood.'

'Oh, thanks for that. I suppose you're hoping for a sensational story.'

Jane improvised. '*Young Woman Enters Strange Cave and Is Never Seen Again.*'

'Oh, shut up. I'll have to go now. I'll speak to you later.' Anna had imagined Jane's familiar grin as she ended the call.

Now, after leaving the Notario's office, she rounded a corner and bumped into Maggie.

'Oh, Anna, I was going to call you this week. Time for a latte?'

'Always,' said Anna as they crossed the road to a pavement café and sat down under a sunshade.

'What's new?' Maggie asked. 'I haven't seen you since we went to see the fortune teller that night. I want to arrange another girls' night out.'

'Well, I've got news. I've just come from the Notarios and my building's been officially condemned and there's compensation.'

'Hooray!' I told you,' said Maggie, 'but you are still staying with Nils, aren't you?'

'Yes,' said Anna wryly, 'we're like an old married couple. By the way, speaking of the fortune teller; did any of her predictions come true?'

'Actually yes, the odd thing,' said Maggie, 'but I had a thought the other day; one of the boys used the word *horrorizado* and I remembered us talking about it that night because your gypsies had used it. You thought it meant something horrible and I said it translated as petrified and we ended up with a cave and a lady who was paralysed with fear, but petrified can also mean, turned to stone. Gypsies are very superstitious, perhaps they think the cave or its surroundings represent something else, something turned to stone.'

Anna considered this for a moment. 'I've just spoken to Jane and she thinks it might be a version of Bluebeard's Castle. Do you know that story?'

'Trust Jane!' Maggie laughed. 'So you may be in

danger of either being murdered or turned to stone.'

'I've promised her I'll explore thoroughly and I'll report back to both of you afterwards. Anything for a peaceful life.'

'I'll make a booking for another night out, probably next week, and let you know. That is if you're still alive.' Maggie drained her coffee cup. 'I've time to run you back to Terreno if you're going home, but then I have to get back for the boys.'

'Yes please,' said Anna, 'and there's more news. Nils' ex-wife Eva is not only alive and well; she's even pregnant. I'll tell you in the car.'

***

Anna had decided not to share the news about her apartment block with Nils for the time being; or at least until she knew how much money was involved.

He was on the terrace reading and looked up as the metal gate opened and clanged shut. He had never shown much interest in whether her situation had progressed any further. Also he showed only scant interest in the imminent publication of her book. For much of the time there was a cosy silence between them which Anna had described to Jane as an intimate enjoyment of their privacy and simple way of life. They shared a love of the island's rustic timelessness. Jane had replied, 'spoken like a writer in love', and pretended to put two fingers down her throat.

'The air's fresh today. I love autumn here.' Anna sat down on an old chair.

'How was Palma Nova?'

'The same. Saw a few familiar faces. Called in the

estate office; nothing finalised there yet. I had a coffee with Maggie and she brought me back in the car.'

'Hmm,' said Nils, marking his place and putting his book down. 'I have been thinking; would you like to spend Christmas here or shall I book a hotel for us? I know of two or three wonderful paradors in the countryside, undiscovered by holiday-makers. I wonder, does religion play a part in your Christmas?'

This was one of those questions Anna always felt defensive when answering; like, have you any children, and do you drive?

'You've asked me about this before and I don't know what to say. I went to church when I was growing up and I taught in a church school. I've always loved the Christmas story and doing nativity plays, but I feel guilty for buying into consumerism as I've grown older. That's it. I'd love to stay in a hotel; what's a parador?'

'Ah', said Nils, 'you will have a treat. Paradors are medieval castles, Moorish fortresses, monasteries and palaces offering accommodation. An unmatched combination of history and beauty, always situated where the scenery is spectacular and refurbished to the very highest standards. It will be my present to you for Christmas. Did you know, my name in English is Nicholas? I will be your Santa Claus.'

Anna moved to stand behind him and put her arms around his neck, laying her cheek against his. 'I didn't know about Nils being Nicholas, it's one of my favourite names. I've seen lots of pictures of St. Nicholas and you could just about pass if you grew your beard a bit; my personal saint and Father Christmas.'

Nils continued, 'My forbears, the Vikings, dedicated

their cathedral to St. Nicholas. It stands in Greenland.'

'Well, said Anna, 'I don't know how the Vikings celebrated but we'll have a lovely time; our first Christmas together.'

'We will indeed, and I have decided to share a secret with you. It is known only to myself and I suspect a very small number of others.'

'Oh', said Anna, sitting down again.

'No', said Nils, rising from his seat. 'It is inside, come with me.'

Anna followed him from the terrace, through the living area, through the bedroom and into the bathroom, where he took the key to the wooden door down from its high ledge. She had a fleeting memory of following the Dragon, in her dreams, to the back of his cave where he unlocked a door and revealed unexpected things.

As Nils turned the key in the lock, Anna heard her heart beating, felt her pulse quicken and her mouth go dry. Was it anticipation? Was it fear? Fear of what? She tried to imagine Jane was behind them, bringing up the rear.

Nils unhooked the battery powered lantern, switching it on to give an eerie illumination all around them. He handed Anna a torch with a faltering beam to help her to see the cave floor beneath her feet.

'I have not noticed you wearing your necklace,' he observed in a quiet voice.

'There's a bit of a problem with the catch,' Anna said. Her voice sounded strange to her in the confined space. Nils said nothing more, walking ahead with confident steps.

They passed through the abandoned art materials and miscellaneous boxes, between the bicycles and past the tailor's dummy. Anna saw Nils' distorted reflection pass across the dusty surface of the propped up mirror, like an evil twin. She wanted to speak to relieve the tension she was feeling, but could think of nothing to say. As the space around them narrowed, the black basalt underfoot shone dully in the light from the torch.

They were now going further in than Anna had gone with Jane and she instinctively reached for Nils' hand as fractured illumination flared then disappeared across the surfaces around them. She heard the ticking noise she remembered from before, now sounding more like a pattering as if tiny feet scurried across the rock face in the darkness.

Just as a building claustrophobia began to affect her breathing, it seemed to Anna that the walls of the invisible space beyond their light beams receded; the darkness stretching further away. What had sounded like *tick, tick, tick*, now sounded more like *drip, drip, drip,* in all directions.

The still air was charged with expectancy. Anna wiped fresh beads of perspiration away from her face and neck but her skin still felt damp. Light from the lantern illuminated a corner ahead and she wondered how far they had come.

Nils' voice was close to her ear, 'there are candles here. Humour me and keep your eyes closed until I light them.'

Anna stood very still, head bowed and eyelids pressed tightly together. She heard Nils step away from her and then she heard the scrape of a match and the flare of sulphur repeated again and again. She was aware of Nils' footfall returning and his hand taking hold of hers. He guided her forward. 'Now look.'

She looked. They had entered a small cavern illuminated now by fat church candles arranged roughly in a semi-circle on the ground. Nils raised his lantern higher. Shadows arched around the cavern walls and flickered across Doric columns, fluted and knotted; calcium deposits formed by mineral rain, developing particle by particle over countless years.

From its base in the glow of clustered candles, a pale statue rose to the height of two men. Its shape was unmistakeable, the form and iconic pose of mother and baby, Virgin and child, Mary and Jesus; although the stalagmite itself may have pre-dated them as it grew slowly in the darkness.

The fluid drape of the figure's garments and of the wrapped bundle cradled in its arms was incredible. There was the semblance of a face with serenely smooth features and closed eyes beneath a slight protuberance suggestive of a halo.

Anna stared and stared; words seemed unnecessary.

Nils spoke first. 'Very few people know of her existence. I myself am not religious but there are plenty here who are; my home would become a shrine or a tourist attraction and I wish only to live here quietly and peacefully. Your friends, the Golds, heard of her somehow and saw a commercial opportunity, but I never allowed them access. The gypsies have found her at some time in the past but they keep her secret. Whilst not beyond stealing from the vast wealth of the Roman church they are both superstitious and religious, and although I confess I do not like them, they have their own codes of behaviour and in this, time has proved they can be relied upon.' His hand tightened its grip. 'Anna?'

'It's beautiful,' she whispered.

'You will tell no one. Not the reporter. Look at me, Anna.'

With a stab of disappointment Anna gave her word. She would have to tell Jane something else. She would deny her best friend what could have been the scoop of a lifetime.

Stalactites from the roof of the cavern had formed the shrouded head and shoulders and babe in arms. Stalagmites had risen up to meet them where the gap joined and thickened at the figure's waist, clothing its lower half in fluted calcified folds.

As Anna continued to stare in the candlelight, a choir sang in her head and she imagined the pealing of Christmas bells.

Nils put both arms round her and for a few moments time stopped, except for the surreal drip, drip, drip, in the darkness surrounding them.

CHAPTER 19
THE FIELD OF DREAMS

Holger had reported some sort of family crisis and asked Nils to stand in for him at Mange Tak. A commis chef named Hans and his wife Astrid had been working all day and Nils had agreed to manage the restaurant for the evening service.

Every Autumn, Danes celebrated the huge diversity of apple varieties to be found in their country. When Nils was young only the older variety of Ingrid Marie apples were grown on the farm; now his countrymen in the eastern Jutland town of Ebeltoft held an annual festival where up to three hundred apple varieties were celebrated with apple juice, cider, cakes, brandy, vinegar, schnapps and even apple art, all on offer.

This evening, Mange Tak would welcome its customers with apple inspired dishes, pastries and drinks. On the menu were a choice of chicken, duck or Baltic herring and eggs, all prepared with apples and seasonal accompaniments or served with rye bread and winter salads of apples, greens and nuts. These were followed by a selection of apple tarts, jellies and soufflés. Customers drank apple juice or cider and could expect a complimentary apple schnapps.

When the last diner had been served and only a low hum of conversation filtered through to the bar from the remaining occupied tables, Nils removed his apron and closed the door to the kitchen, leaving the clearing up to the Spanish woman who came in early every morning. He sat at the end of the bar and removed the folded piece of paper from the breast pocket of the blue and white checked shirt he had hurriedly dressed in earlier. He unfolded it slowly, reflecting that this shirt must have hung at the back of the wardrobe since his unplanned coffee with Jane in Dali's.

Now he smoothed out Eva's drawing, laying it on the bar and frowning at it. What had Jane said about it? Nothing he could remember, only that it had been there on the restaurant's back wall for some time. What was it about it that he found unsettling? It wasn't typical of Eva's work, looking more like the efforts of a child, drawn and coloured in with wax crayons. The flowers growing in the foreground looked like lupines, the splashes of red must be poppies. In the background, spires of flowers stood up above the long grass; frilly pink, dots of deep blue; hollyhocks, delphiniums; yellow, mulleins?

He sipped his apple brandy and slowly saw that the small building wasn't painted vertically in two different shades of red as it had first appeared but that its walls were formed of slats of wood with spaces between them. The sloping roof was solid, probably not painted green but covered in a carpet of well-established vegetation.

He swallowed hard, and the brandy burned his throat, resulting in a brief coughing fit. Angel, the barman, looked up from washing glasses and raised his eyebrows, but Nils flicked the back of his hand at him with an irritated gesture and poured more brandy into his glass.

He and Eva had never travelled back to Denmark

together; Eva had never seen the farm and yet the small barn or shed she had sketched was very like one that had haunted Nils' darkest thoughts for years; one constructed of similar-looking louvered slats of wood driven into bare earth, with sides partially open to the elements. It was roofed over and painted Dalarna red. Intended as an animal pen or shelter it had occasionally been used for storage and sat with a few similar constructions in a small disused hayfield on the farm's perimeter.

In his last winter there, Nils had used it to store a surplus of imperfect and damaged apples, intending to sell them for pig-feed. He had not seen the pig farmer in question and in the spring he had moved the rotting and fermenting apples aside to create space. In the half-light that filtered through the wooden slats he had dug into the earth and created a shallow grave for the body of his first wife, Magda.

Restless in mind and body, he had abandoned the failing farm shortly afterwards and headed north towards Skagen, intending to spend some time embracing the lifestyle of the arty community who lived in and around that area.

First he drove all the way to the peninsula that was the northernmost tip of Denmark, the huge sand bar that reached out for five miles into the path of the two warring seas from the Kattegat and the Skagerrak. Flanked by thrashing water he walked out alone, buffeted by the turbulent air and soaked with spray. It felt like the end of the world.

Over the piercing cries of seabirds he screamed his frustrations into the firmament. He railed against the Norse gods of all his forefathers. He cursed the three fates, the white robed goddesses, daughters of Zeus, for bringing his life to this. He fancied he heard them singing with the Sirens, a sound like no other, as his blood pounded in his veins.

He knelt exhausted on the packed wet sand as if in prayer then rose and turning his back on the peninsula and on his past, he strode forward to seek his future.

He stayed for a while with a Norwegian woman whose piercings he could remember but whose name he could not recall, until one day he found himself thinking of happier times on the island of Mallorca and planned a voyage to take him to the Island of the Pines. He told himself he did not need a woman; nor did he need any reminders of his former life.

Whilst attending university, he had been betrayed by his first love and his best friend. Embittered and disillusioned he had married eventually not for love but to acquire a farmer's wife. At that time the farm still ran a dairy. Magda had experience of this and was able to help his mother but what Nils wanted most of all, a family, sons, was not forthcoming.

As the passage of time saw the loss of first one parent then the other, Nils coped less and less well. Magda had become little more than a liability and his mother, who had always been the special person in his life, had withdrawn from him, even failing to recognise him towards the end. He understood this as a symptom of her condition but felt abandoned nevertheless. Helping to ease both her and his father into the afterlife had been so easy that he found himself contemplating ridding himself of Magda in the same way. Women could never be relied upon to know their place and function in it satisfactorily.

Magda's previous family had no use for her, not even keeping in touch, and now neither did he. She even failed to place any value on her own life, claiming a medical textbook of aches and pains, sleeplessness and depression, nagging and complaining from dawn till dusk.

He considered the same concoctions he had used before and not wishing to be reminded of his mother's death, favoured the first, henbane, belladonna.

He had recently read a book about the infamous American doctor and homeopathic physician, Dr Crippen, who had settled in England before successfully killing his wife by the same means in 1910. Nils had been impressed until reading how the doctor later exposed himself by his own carelessness and had been hanged. Then he felt contempt; he would never be so careless.

The year was 1988 and Nils had had enough. Production on the farm was underfunded and old fashioned. He had tried to modernise but failed to make things profitable within the bounds of what he considered to be ethical. He had become massively disheartened and frustrated with how the country was being governed and how farming in general was becoming more intensive, relying more and more on hazardous chemicals which could only upset the balance of nature.

He grieved for the seas around Denmark, which had suffered an unprecedented catalogue of modern disasters, their ecology collapsing with contamination. In 1984, the *Dana Optima*, a ship flying the Danish flag, had lost her cargo of dinitrophenol, a herbicide banned in America for causing reproductive failure in mammals. It lay deep in the North Sea, its containers slowly corroding.

In this year of 1988 there had been a series of catastrophes: a mystery illness devastated fifty per cent of the population of harbour seals in the Baltic and Wadden seas: a mystery fire on the Piper Alpha oil rig claimed one hundred and sixty seven lives whilst doing untold damage to marine life, but worst of all was the sudden blooming of algae, chrysochromulina polylepis, on the waters of the Skagerrak and the Kattegat. This released a lethal poison along one thousand kilometres of the coast-lines of Norway and Denmark. It killed marine life and marine life killed people. Fish and shellfish stored poisons in their flesh which formed the basic diet of most Scandinavians.

So many people had died tragically that Nils reasoned one more death would make little difference and, if need be, could be attributed to a dish of contaminated mussels, a favourite food of Magda's.

The memories which resurfaced around the time of the apple festivals were always unwelcome, although he prided himself on having treated Magda's body with respect, if not exactly reverence. As her husband he had wanted her to remain on the farm and her body had been buried there in a sheltered field under a sheltering roof.

Afterwards, he had felt more gloomy than ever, all of life seeming polluted. It had not been difficult to pack some belongings and leave for Skagen and an uncertain future. However, he respected order and discipline too much and quickly realised the Bohemian lifestyle was not for him; although perversely his senses were to be seduced again by Eva, who was of the same free-thinking ilk.

He had been becoming more successful at distancing

himself from all of this until Erik had decided he wanted the farm and its lands to be sold. Returning for the first time had brought everything back.

He carefully re-folded Eva's drawing and returned it to his pocket. Everyone had left the restaurant and Nils suddenly realised Angel was waiting to lock up. He discovered he was a little unsteady on his feet but the barman knew better than to query the wisdom of his employer driving home under the influence of a surfeit of apple brandy. They wished each other a formal 'goodnight'.

'You're very late. Was it a good night? Was the restaurant busy?' Anna went to kiss him as he entered the cave-house. 'What a strong smell of apples.'

'I'll shower and change.'

'No, I like it. It's a lovely sweet smell. It smells of summer.'

'Hmm.' Nils went towards the kitchen. 'Would you like coffee?'

Anna followed him. 'You know I've never seen you putting on aftershave and I don't think I've ever seen any in the bathroom but there's always a masculine scent of something about you. I've been thinking about Christmas presents and I've no idea what it is you use.'

'I use only the organically produced soap which is kept in the cabinet.' Nils poured freshly boiled water over ground coffee beans.

'Oh, how odd,' said Anna. 'Sometimes I think you smell of the sea, you know, sort of a clean briny tang, and other times I can smell apples, like now only not as strong.'

‘I must bring it on my clothes from the restaurant. You have an acute sense of smell.’

‘Thank you’, Anna said playfully, ‘and you have a cute beard.’

‘Come and sit beside me and I will tell you a Christmas story for December the thirteenth.’ Nils carried their coffees to a settee which had a thick imitation fur throw over it, grey with white shading. Anna said it made her think of reindeers, although she confessed to never having seen a real one.

‘Are you familiar with Saint Lucia?’

Anna shook her head and settled down, arranging the throw around them.

‘Perhaps you should be. I believe she is, among other things, a patron saint of writers.’

‘Really? I suppose I need to know about her then.’

‘Her name, Lucia, means light. She was a Neapolitan saint, recognised by various Christian denominations and especially celebrated in Sweden. Danes adopted her to bring light to the darkness during the German occupation in the Second World War. Hitler was defeated and we kept Saint Lucia. On December the twelfth, the eve of Saint Lucia’s day, Danes switch off electric lights and burn candles instead. We observe this tradition in the restaurant and it is a magical night. You must be there.’

‘Oh, I think I’ve seen something about that on television; a parade. Do people carry candles and someone is Lucia and wears a wreath of fir and candles like a crown?’

Nils nodded. ‘Just so. Scandinavian schools and universities hold this celebration before beginning the holidays.’

'I remember now, we discussed doing something with that tradition a few years ago in the school where I worked in England but there were too many health and safety issues with the candles and it wasn't the same without real ones. Aren't there special Lucia buns to eat as well?'

'Indeed, they represent her eyes. She is also patron saint of the blind.'

'Why is that?'

'She was sainted for refusing to marry a pagan, resulting in either her eyes being gouged out as a form of torture prior to her execution or, in the alternative version, some say she removed them herself in defiance of her persecutors. She is depicted in art carrying them on a plate.'

Anna squirmed beneath the throw, drawing her knees up and squeezing her eyes shut. 'I really wish you hadn't told me that; it's made me feel a bit sick.'

Nils smiled his half smile. 'You have no need to worry. You are not going to refuse to marry anyone who is a pagan . . . are you?'

***

The Dragon had been drifting through Nils' unconscious mind and paused to listen to the story with interest. He remembered Lucia being very unhappy, but had always been mystified by the human classification of 'saint' with reference to another human. He supposed they were some kind of god but was puzzled as to where they resided. They did not exist in the ice and mists of Niflhel, the realms for the undistinguished dead, but neither were they

in Valhalla with heroes slain in battle.

He was also puzzled by the significance of the stalagmite column in the cave but understood it was related to a religious character and must be respected. He did know it was some sort of icon and that Anna would have to be made aware of its existence before she could be fully accepted in the cave-house with Nils. At last this had been achieved; now the story could progress.

He anticipated the journeys he would take Anna on in her dreams. The two of them would be collaborators in the fulfilment of his mission here.

All mortals faced a death but the Dragon knew the cycle of life never ended and as long as the sun warmed the planet and the clouds released their rain, he would be immortal, while all humans would meet their fates eventually.

He knew Nils had not forgotten Magda, but he had not gone to the farm and would not have visited her resting place if he had; however, Nils would have to face his demons soon, and Magda's wronged spirit was waiting.

***

Magda's life had been filled with disappointment. The man she had fallen in love with had offered her a marriage which would provide security and a lifestyle she could relate to. She was well used to farm work and looked forward to raising a family, but there had been no family and her husband expected her to undertake a heavy workload with few rewards.

Romance and affection had been short-lived. Her

overalls were always dirty, her boots covered in mud. She had no time to wash her long dark hair, which had once been so admired; now she kept it plaited around her head and her husband barely looked at her. More and more of her time was taken nursing her elderly mother and father-in-law. They had been kind to her and she had tried to do her best for them but work on the farm had meant they were each left alone for long periods of time.

Eventually Herr Christiansen had had a merciful release; his wife suffered more and her death had been distressing; Magda had felt very sad. She was left tired and lonely and was only thirty two years old when she died un-mourned, her body buried without ceremony.

Now her bones were frozen by winter snows and thawed in the spring; chilled at night and warmed by the sun in the daytime. She had seeped all her secrets and sorrows into the soil. The soil had passed them on to the whispering grasses. They had soaked little by little into the timber frame around them where the wood was soft and damp and rotting. Wild flowers had grown up, opened to release them on sunny days, and small creatures, soft little field mice and birds of the field and forest, had carried them away in seeds, even as far as the clapboard farmhouse which still stood, backed by a stand of dark leafy trees. The wood there was rotting too now. The farmhouse had been painted beneath the overhanging thatch with Dalarna red, the wood preservative seen on so many Scandinavian buildings, but here it had long since lost its vibrancy and the colour resembled that of old dried blood. Through a broken window pane, tattered fabric flapped uselessly and the wind made an unearthly whistling noise. The black cloven hooves of red deer picked their way daintily past the weathered front porch, past a few straggling roses, choked by prickly sow-thistle and overtaken by ground elder.

The Danish style of design, simple, effective and beautiful, was left to nature to achieve. It had made colourful headway here and there with a profusion of bindweed, oxeye daisies, nettles, poppies and the yellow flowered great mulleins. Some of the fields were blue with lupines.

CHAPTER 20
BROUGHT TO BOOK

The late January air was crisp and invigorating with ozone and tar from the harbour, with exhaust fumes and the smell of fresh coffee drifting from the streets and terraces, and with air from hot ovens and aromas of freshly baked goods from the panaderías.

Shop-owners refurbished and painted; hoteliers renewed and polished before wooing their clientele with special offers. Real estate agents sharpened their wits and sorted through their lists of clients and empty properties, hoping to marry one with the other.

Short days faded into early evenings with bright starry skies and the tantalising promise of anything-could-happen tomorrows.

***

The Dragon crouched on the terrace, a satisfied smile curving the corners of his thin lips. He was reading Anna's mind as she wrote an overdue letter to her friend and agent. Her aura shone bright and positive. His work here was almost done, but he would return years from now to this location or to wherever life had taken these mortals, in order to observe their situations.

He had seen into Anna's life; seen her childhood, her schooldays, her birthdays and Christmases. He

knew her favourite foods, games, clothes and pastimes. He saw her parents. He saw her future here in this place and that fate would be gentle with her. She would have bad luck and good luck in equal measures.

Anna had been a tool, a vehicle he had used to achieve his ends, but he had relished their nightly journeys together. These had increased in variety and intensity as Anna's new manuscript began to take shape. As the year turned, he had seen she was becoming more in tune with her senses, more receptive of the stimuli which were all around her, drawing inspiration from the things he showed her. Now she fell asleep and waited for her muse and mentor to appear in the shadowy hinterland of her dreams.

He had taken her north to his homelands. From as far away as Greenland they passed over the land of the Vikings whose genes were carried by Nils, but who had been denied the chance to carry them further. Long Viking shadows undulated across bare landscapes like a herd of stampeding beasts, their war-cries echoing down the years.

To embed a feel for northern lands and cultures he had shown her fantastic creatures, both real and of myth and legend.

Around Greenlandic waters they had seen the lonely shambling shapes of polar bears keeping their offspring close; all dirty cream against the blinding white. And from above the ocean they saw the spouts of whales, the dorsal fins of dolphins slipping under the waves and, occasionally, the blunt noses and long

spiral tusks of narwhals, the unicorns of the sea.

He had shown her sea serpents and ghost ships with pirate crews. They had glimpsed the lithe bodies and silvery tails of merfolk and seen shipwrecks on the ocean floor, with drowned bells which could be heard tolling mournfully in the silt of the seabed. They had heard seals singing; believed by some to be enchanted royalty, sons and daughters of the King of Scandinavia, and by others to be singing the song of the drowned.

They often found themselves in the fields and fens of Jutland; sometimes in an overgrown field with small faded red shelters where the surface vegetation was alive with sound and movement. If it was summer as they brushed by, the mechanical rattling as hundreds of blue lupines suddenly fired small black seeds from their seed-pods made Anna start with surprise. Sometimes it was winter and many things lay dormant underground waiting for spring to bring them back to life. Other things merely remained, reanimated only by the slow process of decay.

As they passed across Europe, the snow of Scandinavia changed to the snow of the Spanish Pyrenees. They saw, under cover of darkness, peasant children leaving out food for the monachicchi, the spirits of children who had died unbaptised, whose cold baby fingers reached out to touch those who came their way in the olive groves at night.

They witnessed processions winding their way through old graveyards to celebrate El Día De Los Muertos, The Day of the Dead.

The world of the Dragon was peopled with such

things, things which celebrated connections between life and the afterlife and he relished opportunities to share them. In this case, they would soon gain an even wider audience.

***

Meanwhile, Anna's letter was growing longer.

***

Hi Sue,

Have just opened your last email, sent yesterday, thanks, and decided to scribble a really long letter to catch up.

I owe you a million thanks for getting my last story out there. I know it's early days but, as you know, everything looks really promising.

Who would have thought, when we were at school together all those years ago, that you would become a successful literary agent one day and I would become a successful writer? You've always been a good friend but your support's been invaluable to me.

Please try to visit this year, there's so much I want to show you and, of course, I want you to meet Nils. Guess what, he proposed to me at Christmas and I said 'yes' so perhaps you could make it to the wedding. I'll keep you posted on that one; it'll be later this year after his divorce from the mysterious Eva has been finalised.

Also I'm still waiting for some compensation for the apartment to come through from the decision makers in the county hall in Calvia. Anything like this takes an absolute age here. I don't even know what the amount will be yet; fingers crossed for fair play from them.

Meanwhile, the publishers have queried the possibility of there being more stories in the pipeline, another three even, but I've got a different idea and I want to run it by you. Can't believe I'm even in a position to make choices!!!

I'd like to try and move on from children's stories and try a sort of murder mystery for adults, but still with fairy-tale characters, kind of.

I began making notes towards the end of last year, in fact soon after I moved in here really. I could have a very early draft ready this summer if you could find time to give it a read-through. I'll include an outline in this letter so you have some idea of what I'm talking about.

I know it sounds corny but I've been inspired by Nils. He doesn't like to talk about his previous life, before he came here, but he's actually a very interesting person; being a bit older than me he's had lots of experiences. I think I absorb a lot from his feelings. I've become fascinated by the whole Norse mythology, Viking, Danish thing. I'd love to visit Denmark and he's said we can go for a holiday after we get married. Have you ever been? Nils has a younger brother in Copenhagen, but it's a bit complicated.

Anyway, I've been having these incredible dreams. It's hard to explain but they're a bit like flying; like going to Neverland with Peter Pan, or like Charles Dickens' ghosts of Christmas. (Don't laugh, I'm serious.)

It must be something to do with knowing Nils, because I see Scandinavia a lot, especially Denmark. Did I tell you, he sailed here in the eighties on his own, in his own boat? Apparently, most Danes are sailors.

I imagine sea monsters and there's a dragon, there's always a dragon; they live in the sea off the coast of Denmark, by the way! Actually I only managed to describe the dragon in my last story after I'd met Nils and been to his cave-house last summer. After that I seemed to finish the book quite quickly. I don't think I ever told you that.

I know I told you he part-owns a restaurant and we go there about once a week. He spends a bit of his time working there and the rest of the time he writes papers for some Scandinavian institute and for some journal associated with the university in Copenhagen. He writes about the ecology of the sea and about naturally and organically sourced foods and medicinal things. It's all interesting stuff, especially the food, but some of it's in Danish and some of it's way over my head.

So I don't read what he's writing about and he doesn't read what I'm writing either. We give each other space and everything works quite well.

Did I tell you he grew up on a farm? Well, he's just sold the land so I'll never see it now but I think he must have described a bit of it to his ex-wife because she was an artist and she drew a picture of it and I've seen the picture and it was just how I'd imagined it too, bizarre! The whole landscape and the trees and flowers and some sheds or something.

Sorry for rambling on about Nils, you have to come and meet him.

Anyway, as I said, I've plotted the rough outline of my story and I need your feedback. Early (very) draft to follow in the summer if you like the sound of it.

A man commits a murder (or more than one- I haven't decided) which then goes undetected for years. The man moves away from his past and starts a new life, but as he gets older he becomes haunted by various strange creatures, mythical ones, that urge him to confess; then they're joined by ghosts of his ancestors (quite a party), some of whom justify and even glorify killing.

He lives with this dilemma, a sort of struggle with his conscience and morality and meanwhile the reader is wondering where the body is and whether it will be found before the man is driven to confess or whether the whole thing will remain buried (excuse the pun) and the man will take his secret to his own grave. Or . . . will he murder again? Does he find killing too easy? Necessary even?

There's a bit more to it than that as someone begins to follow him, or is he just being paranoid? Actually, I haven't decided this bit yet but I do need another protagonist. I haven't decided who to base this character on yet but it'll come to me, (it might even be me!).

I've based my main character on Nils because he's such a strong character and the most interesting person I know. My head's so full of stuff about Denmark that I've buried the body there in a field on a farm. I'm using the pictures in my head to describe it all in detail. Nils wouldn't mind because he's moved on from his farm and now it's sold anyway. I think the land's going to have pigs rooting around on it soon.

I won't ask him to read any of it because he's not really interested. I'll wait until it achieves publication (with your help), if it does; then I'll surprise him.

So, this will be my first proper novel; what do you think?

Lots of love,
Anna.

Lightning Source UK Ltd.
Milton Keynes UK
UKOW05f1707260813

215996UK00001B/72/P